the
hatchet
man

Mel Arrighi **the hatchet man**

New York and London

Harcourt Brace Jovanovich

Printed in the United States of America

Library of Congress Cataloging in Publication Data

Arrighi, Mel.
    The hatchet man.

    I. Title.
PZ4.A775Hat [PS3551.R7]   813'.5'4   75–12584
ISBN 0–15–139232–3

First edition

B C D E

the
hatchet
man

one

1 My second night back in town, I went up to Pablo's.

I had spent a winter's retreat in the woods, to "get my head together," as the current phrase had it. It had been a fine and purifying experience, but I had returned to New York with a sense of uneasiness. I feared that I might have been away too long, might have missed out on something. And so I hastened to check in, to reclaim my set-aside life.

Pablo smiled when he saw me. "How's the country, Don?" he asked.

"It's great if you're a robin. I'm back in town. To rest up from all that peace and quiet."

I took in the place. It seemed even dingier than I remembered, and, with its corny Cuban cantina look, even tackier. But, as always, each table in the long front room had its media star, some favored journalist, novelist, or screenwriter. I moved toward the small, empty table by the window.

"That's reserved, Don."

I turned and looked at him. It struck me that everything about Pablo was a little brighter than usual, his smile, his button eyes, the sheen on his fat, sweaty face.

"It's where I always sit," I said.

"It's reserved. I've a table for one in the back room," he suggested helpfully.

The back room at Pablo's was the wasteland, the most the nonpeople could aspire to, but something a regular only saw on his way to the lavatory.

"It's not just for myself," I said, misunderstanding our impasse. "I'm expecting a lady."

"I'll send her on back."

I was suddenly aware that the choice tables had gone silent. I glanced around. At the next table, Jerry Gutman was sitting with a couple of his cronies. He was faced away from me, but that didn't mean he was missing anything. Like many political reporters, Jerry had cultivated the art of listening with his back.

"What about that table over there?" I asked, pointing to an empty table at the rear.

"Reserved," Pablo said.

Jerry Gutman turned around in his chair. His shrewd, bearded face softened with a compassionate smile. "You want to join us, Don?"

"No, thanks." I raised my voice slightly, enough so that my words would carry, but not so much that I would seem to be losing my cool. "I don't think I want to eat at this low-grade diner. I've seen the kitchen."

I heard one of the nonpeople at the bar chuckle, a sympathetic, comradely chuckle. I had joined the club.

"Suit yourself," Pablo said.

Outside, I let the crisp April wind cool my face. Welcome back to reality, I thought.

My winter in the woods had disoriented me. When I lost my column, I had followed my first impulse and taken an out-of-season rental in Vermont, an old farmhouse, the perfect place to write a novel. Soon the city and its life seemed as vanished as a pond under ice. But when the thaw came I had assumed it would all be as it was before.

Of course not. Nothing had paused in my absence. I was back, not reborn, but simply redefined—a cashiered journalist, out of demand, professionally nowhere. Pablo, that nicely calibrated instrument, had measured me exactly. A back-room number.

There was a public phone booth on the corner. I went into it and looked up the number of WMCA. I called the radio station and left a message for Sally—I wouldn't be meeting her later, I didn't feel well, I was going home to go to bed.

I hung up, left the booth, and started walking along East Fiftieth Street. I crossed Fifth Avenue and passed by the Rockefeller Center skating rink. Up ahead, in front of the RCA Building, there was more than the usual bustle in the street. Limousines. Plump penguins and slinky silvered seals. The moneyed set. An Event had taken place.

I paused across the street from the main entrance of the building and watched the people going in and out. Huge, naked, stone figures topped the entrance, classic figures with tiny penises and pneumatic breasts, representing some mythic thing or the other. The flesh-and-blood people, in tuxedos and evening gowns, passing underneath seemed doll-like by comparison, and a little foolish in their self-importance.

I tried to remember what was going on. It had been announced in the paper that day, and, after a moment, it came to me. There was a grandiose testimonial dinner in the Rainbow Room for some top city official.

I walked on. At the intersection on Sixth Avenue, on the two far corners, chanting demonstrators pressed against police lines. The group to the south of Fiftieth Street was chanting one thing, the group to the north something else. They fused only in a common note of rage, an ecstatic rage that meant the Mayor was somewhere nearby.

At the near corner, a crowd of people was pouring out of Radio City Music Hall. Tourists, suburbanites, pimply teen-age couples. They chatted happily among themselves and totally ignored the screaming pandemonium across the street from them.

I asked a policeman who the demonstrators were. "Those are the teachers," he said, pointing to the southerly group, "and the queers are over there."

The teachers were, for the most part, bearded and shabby as Mexican bandits. The Gay Lib crowd on the north corner looked neat as accountants. I laughed.

Horrible city, I thought, as I walked on, grotesque, doomed, and, God, how I'd missed it! Night warblers and barking dogs on sleeping farms were no substitute for the cry of the crazies in Manhattan streets. I had been kidding myself with the Thoreau bit. In any time, there is only one heart to the carnival; and everywhere else is for dropouts and other such completed stories.

I hailed a cab and went down to the Village. Back in my apartment, I set up the bucket of ice and the bottle of Scotch beside my bed, undressed, slipped in between the sheets, downed a Tuinal with my first swallow of the Scotch, picked up the TV remote control and switched on the late news.

The handsome anchorman looked out at me and mouthed his copy. Submissively, I let his unblinking gaze capture me, although, with the sound off, I had no idea what he was saying.

The image changed to another, equally handsome young man, standing in the lobby of a large building. Men and women in evening clothes streamed by in the background. After a few moments, I realized it was the lobby of the RCA Building. These were the guests departing from the testimonial dinner.

An attractive couple entered the frame. The reporter squared off with the man and began interviewing him. The mike passed back and forth between them. But it was the woman who held my attention. She was young, blonde, and expensively beautiful. Beyond that, she was maddeningly familiar.

I tried, for one foggy moment, to place her. But the Tuinal was dulling my brain.

She lifted her gaze and looked out between the two profiles. Her smile brightened with light surprise, as if she had just then noticed me lying there in bed. "Good night, beautiful lady," I whispered, and switched off the set. The picture shrunk swiftly to a point of light, then went to nothing. And so did I.

2   The alarm hadn't yet gone off. It was the phone that was ringing.

I grabbed for the receiver. "Hello?"

"Mr. Skelton?" It was a cheery girl secretary's voice. "Blake Hivnor calling."

Blake Hivnor was the editor in chief of *View*. A call from him was supposed to make a free-lance writer's heart beat faster. But when Hivnor came on the line I wasn't all that excited. I was still too groggy from the pill.

"Don? How are you?"

"Fine, thanks, Blake."

"I saw you at Pablo's last night. Sorry you didn't stay. I wanted to talk with you."

"Yeah, well, I suddenly remembered I was supposed to be someplace else."

"How *is* your schedule?" he asked.

"Busy."

"Will you be in town this next month?"

"I imagine so." I waited a moment, then inquired casually, "You've got something in mind?"

"Yeah. A profile on Penelope Wren."

"Of course!" I said.

"What do you mean—'of course'?"

"Sorry, pay no attention. I just remembered I saw her on the late news last night."

"That's right. She and her husband were at the Rainbow Room."

"Beautiful girl," I commented.

"Isn't she, though? I want a long, in-depth piece on her."

"Does she rate the space?"

"She will after her movie opens. She's sensational in it. You free for lunch tomorrow?"

"Sure."

"Italian Pavilion. One o'clock. All right?" There was a silence at his end as he wrote it down. "There's a special slant I want for this article," he said. "You know much about politics, Don?"

"I vote. Sometimes."

He laughed. "That's good enough. We'll talk about it at lunch. See you tomorrow." He hung up.

The alarm went off. It was nine o'clock.

I got up, padded into the kitchen, and turned on the flame under the pot of leftover coffee. I poured a lukewarm cup of it, went into the living room, sat in the armchair by the front window, and gazed out at West Eleventh Street.

It was a schizoid view. When it was clear and sunny, the unbroken flock of flaking brownstones was heart-rending in its charm; a glimpse into the more gracious world that had died before I was born. On a gray day, it seemed a depressing slum. It was dark and overcast this morning.

I pondered Blake Hivnor's parting question about politics. Penelope Wren, as an ornament at least, was very much part of the political scene. Her father was James Wren, the former Senator from New York. And her husband was, if I remembered correctly, a city official, one of the Mayor's bright young men. Fine, but what did all that have to do with her acting career and her motion-picture debut?

Well, whatever Hivnor's angle was, I'd find out soon enough. Until then, there was no point in thinking about it. The fact was, I wasn't too interested. There was a time when landing a new assignment would have charged me up with excitement. But no longer. I had been overexposed.

In the past five years, I had captured the distilled essences of forty-one egocentrics—actors, singers, film directors, playwrights—in long profiles in the major magazines and short pieces in the Sunday *Times*. There are only so many times you can step into a stranger's life, unwelcome but asked for, relating with the sour intensity of a brief, loveless copulation, before you feel a certain ennui. At the age of thirty-two, I was losing my taste for people, celebrated or otherwise.

The telephone rang again. It was Sally Fry. "How are you?" she asked.

"How am I?" I echoed, puzzled for a moment. Then I remembered the message I had left for her at the radio station. "Oh, I feel much better," I assured her. "I guess it was just some bug that hit me. How did it go last night?"

"As well as could be expected," she said, a bit grimly. Sally had played nursemaid to a movie-star client who had appeared on a radio talk show. It was the least favorite of her duties.

"Did he stay sober?"

"No. But he managed to be coherent. Barely." She paused. "I called a little while ago. Your line was busy." It was none of her business. But Sally never could resist her curiosity.

"I was talking to an editor. Blake Hivnor."

"Blake Hivnor!" Her tone was appropriately impressed. "Does he want you to do something for *View?*"

"Yeah. A piece on Penelope Wren."

"That's terrific! We handle her."

"Well, what do you know," I murmured. It wasn't all that marvelous a coincidence. The P.R. firm Sally worked for was the leader in its field; it represented most of the younger movie stars. "Why has she gone to the trouble of hiring you? I thought Miss Wren didn't seek out personal publicity."

"We don't just promote," Sally said cryptically. "We protect." There was a silence. Then she asked, in a wary tone, "This isn't going to be one of your hatchet jobs, is it, Don?"

"What kind of thing is *that* to ask? I thought you loved me."

"I love you, but I know your work."

The line made me wince. Love in the Media. It was like a courting dance on sword blades.

It had been different in Vermont, when Sally had come up to be with me, and we had lain in each other's arms through the pure quiet of snowfall nights. Then we had dreamed of marriage, of children, of all the usual things. But now we were back in New York, returned to the context of our respective occupations, and everything was maneuver again. Cynical suspicion came first, love was an afterthought, and our innocent winter dreams seemed meaningless.

"Don't worry," I said. "I may not even do this."

"Why not?"

"Well, it would be sort of a regression for me. I wasn't going to do any more of these pieces."

"That's for you to decide." In the background, I heard her other phone ring. "I can't talk any longer, darling," she said, suddenly brisk. "Call me tonight."

"I will."

"Love you." She hung up.

I knew that my show of reluctance hadn't convinced her. I'd be regressing, all right. But who was I kidding? My career was in trouble. I knew it, Sally knew it, and Blake Hivnor knew it.

A big assignment for *View* would put me back on the track, of course. But, rather than being hopeful, I felt suddenly uneasy. Hivnor hadn't ever called when things were going well for me. Why was he calling me now, when I was so desperate I was ready to do just about anything?

I suspected his timing wasn't accidental. And I already had a premonition of trouble.

3 We hewed to the ritual of the publishing lunch. Serious business was put off until dessert and coffee. The time, up to then, was filled with pleasantries and trade gossip.

Blake Hivnor wasn't much for small talk and I did most of the work. It was unsettling to talk to him. He listened like an editor. He heard just those things he found really interesting or that might possibly be useful. The rest was sidetracked to some slush pile of unreceived communication.

"Beautiful, terrific," he murmured, after I mentioned the sudden passing away of a beloved, elderly lady agent. I was confused for a moment, then I realized he thought I had reached the punch line of a humorous anecdote I had actually completed a couple of minutes before.

I gave up on the bright chitchat and poked at the *mousse au chocolat* that had just been placed before me. Blake tapped his vanilla ice cream absently, his eyes wandering about the restaurant, picking out the details of the pattern of interrelationships—between editors, agents, writers, publicists—in that frozen moment of the lunch whirl. Then his gaze focused on the mirrored wall as he studied the reflections of the new arrivals coming down the steps into the dining room.

Blake Hivnor was not yet forty, delicately built, fairhaired, and pink-skinned. He had been editor in chief of *View* for not much more than a year. But, in that year, he had transformed it from an arthritic granny to something bright, frolicsome, with a cutting edge.

Blake broke the silence. "I like your work, Don," he said

abruptly, without preamble. "You're the kind of writer I want for my magazine."

"I dig your magazine," I said, a curtsey to his bow. "It's the kind I want to write for."

"When I took over," he went on, "the magazine was top-heavy with contributing editors. I've been phasing out the old dodderers. Now I have some room for new, young writers." He paused. "It all depends on how your first couple of pieces work out, of course. But there's no harm in looking ahead to the future. So, tell me, would you consider going under exclusive contract?"

I faked a moment of thoughtful hesitation. "I'd consider it, yes."

My cool was impeccable. But, all the while, I was wondering if Blake had any real idea of the bad shape I was in.

He knew I had lost my column, of course. And he knew about the libel suit that had led to its being dropped. It had been hot gossip in the trade at the time.

Beyond that, I was having my problems as a free lance. Paradoxically, the better known I had become the less in demand I was. Somewhere along the way I had acquired an Image. I saw myself as an honest reporter; others saw me as a hatchet man. There had been flak and retaliation, and the big magazines had grown leery of using me.

So a contributing editor's setup with *View* looked good to me. It wasn't simply the prestige, the money. Conceivably, it could mean my very survival in the field.

But I wasn't about to count on it. The word was that Blake's verbal contracts were as good as the paper they were written on.

"Maybe we should take one thing at a time," I said. "Let's talk about Penelope Wren. You want a long profile, right?"

"Five thousand words," he replied. "If it justifies running longer, I'll give you the space."

"Forgive me for asking, but are there five thousand words that can be said about this girl?"

"I think so."

I was perplexed. "As far as I can see, Penelope Wren is a clean-living WASP princess with some possibilities as a movie star. And that's all there is to her."

"Your story isn't just Penelope."

"Who else, then? Her father? He's a figure out of the fifties. No one would be interested now."

"I'm not talking about the Senator. I mean Elliot Karp."

Elliot Karp was Penelope's husband. I had already done some homework, and I knew that Karp was one of the glamour boys of the Mayor's administration. He bore the resounding title Director of the Agency for Urban Development.

"So what's your angle?" I asked. "Penelope as the public servant's loyal, invaluable wife?"

"Not exactly."

"A conflict angle? Can the Mayor's bright young man," I intoned, improvising a blurb, "accept his wife in her new role as cinema sex goddess?"

"Pretty schlocky, Don." He chuckled. It was the first thing I had said that really amused him.

"Well, for Christ's sake, give me a clue!"

"Clue number one. This bright young man is not so bright."

"This is earth-shattering news? The Mayor is no mental giant, either."

"Perhaps not." He paused meaningfully. "But the Mayor is honest."

"And Elliot Karp?"

Blake didn't choose to answer me directly. "He came out of nowhere. He married Penelope, set up his shingle as a professional son-in-law, and he was rolling. He was a big wheeler-dealer in the Mayor's campaign. I don't think Karp helped much in getting him elected, but the Mayor was glad to have him, anyway. He's got the presidential itch and James Wren still has a lot of clout at a party convention. The Urban Development appointment was a political payoff, of course."

"What's this about honesty?" I asked. "Does Karp have his hand in the till?"

"Maybe." He shrugged. "I don't know."

"Okay, let's say there *is* some hanky-panky going on. You don't expect me to work that into a profile on Penelope Wren, do you?"

"I don't see why not."

"Wait a minute. Who am I doing this piece on, anyway?"

"I told you, your story is Elliot Karp."

"You mean this Penelope Wren thing is just camouflage?"

"You wouldn't get Karp's story if you went straight at him, would you? So you go ahead as if you really *were* doing an article with that charming angle you mentioned—Penelope as the public servant's loyal, invaluable wife."

This was a very different picture and I didn't know if I liked it. A standard profile on a rising young actress was one thing. A hatchet job on one of the Mayor's trusted lieutenants was something else again.

"You say this guy is a grafter?"

"He's a natural con man," Blake said. "No man is a little bit crooked—any more than a girl is a little bit pregnant. Karp is bound to be consistent. So check out what he's been up to at the Urban Development office."

"You have anything tangible to go on?"

"Nothing tangible." Blake smiled pensively. "I don't know why it is, Don, but when it comes to smelling out a phony, I never miss. It worries me sometimes."

At that point, I wasn't questioning his nose for dishonesty. I was wondering about his editorial judgment. Corrupt municipal officials were nothing new, after all.

Of course, the Penelope Wren connection gave it some

national interest. And, perhaps most significantly, the Mayor himself had become a national figure.

As did most liberal New Yorkers, I rather liked the Mayor. I sometimes deplored his obtuseness, but I responded to his style and respected his good intentions. He was a credible presidential prospect. But first he had to be re-elected Mayor.

"What have you got against the Mayor, Blake?" I asked.

He seemed a bit surprised by the question. "Nothing," he replied. "I think he's sweet. Why do you ask?"

"Just wondering. If you publish a scandal about Elliot Karp—with the primaries coming up—the Mayor is finished."

Blake shrugged. "That's the breaks. Now, about Karp," he went on briskly. "There's one very important thing—check out his background. Don't take any of it at face value. Confirm every detail."

"You expecting something?"

"It's only a hunch. But I have a feeling that if you dig into Elliot Karp deep enough, you'll discover he's just a figment of his own imagination."

"I'm sure he was thoroughly investigated before he was given his appointment."

"I know for a fact he wasn't."

"That's hard to believe."

"Is it really?" Blake regarded me pleasantly. My faith in the workings of the system seemed to charm him. "Our Mayor is not only good and pure and upright. He is also a snob. He would never dream of investigating James Wren's son-in-law. Karp may have started out non-U and a Jew. But, by marriage, he has become an Episcopalian gentleman. The Mayor does not question his own kind."

"Okay, maybe so," I said. "But this is a little off my beat. Why do you think I'm right for this?"

"You're show-business oriented. No one will suspect what you're really after. And you have your peculiar talent. You can flush out more dirty little secrets in less time than any writer I know."

That answered my question, all right. A few more heart-felt compliments like this and I would cut my throat.

"What if I come up with nothing?" I asked. "Where would that leave me?"

"All right, I'll guarantee you this. If you find nothing, if this turns out to be just one of my paranoid fantasies, you can still write your usual kind of profile on Penelope Wren and I'll print it. So what do you have to lose?"

What, indeed? There was nothing left to worry me but my liberal scruples.

Even so, there was something odd about the whole thing, something that didn't jibe. Blake Hivnor was the editor of a national magazine. And yet he was asking me to write an exposé of an individual that no one west of the Hudson had ever heard of. And, if I succeeded, I was likely to destroy the only idealistic mayor New York had had since Fiorello La Guardia.

But who was I to be fastidious? No one was pounding on my door, demanding my services. And this would be a major story in a major magazine. A last-minute reprieve for my career.

"Okay," I said, "I'll give it a try."

two

1   The screening room was packed. The movie was being shown every evening that week, but, still, there wasn't an empty seat in the red-upholstered little hideaway under the Rizzoli bookstore.

Sally, who was seeing the film for the third or fourth time, was somewhat restless. But I was captured by the images, the images of Penelope—Penelope in close-up, filling the wide screen with her mysterious smile; Penelope in long shot, running nude toward a moonlit swimming pool; Penelope in two-shot, lashing out at the man who loved her too incompletely.

She was blonde and very fair, the superhealthy American girl, her body firm and precisely turned—as happens only once in a woman's life, in the interval between baby fat and the soft flesh of maturity. Her features were regular, though a trifle too strong; the mouth was quite full, the nose straight but prominent. Her eyes were extraordinary, very large and brilliant blue.

They had the compelling yet enigmatic gaze I associated with very nearsighted actors. You could not tell whether they were seeing everything or nothing.

Her acting was artless, in the best sense: simple, spontaneous, unstudied. Her relaxation was amazing when you considered that this was a Hermann Dichter film.

Afterward, we went to the Schrafft's on Madison Avenue. It had been recently modernized, transformed from an old-fashioned, wood-paneled ice-cream parlor to a near-replica of a Howard Johnson's, but we still went there after a screening or a play out of force of habit.

As we ate our sundaes, Sally filled me in on the gossip. "Dichter was really horrible to her. You know the kind of thing —yelling at her, ridiculing her in front of the crew, telling her she had no talent."

"Par for the course," I said. "Hermann was just being his usual cuddly self."

"He was worse than ever, they say. Halfway through, he almost fired her."

"For what reason?"

Sally shrugged. "I don't know."

She should have known better than to be telling me this. But to her I was still, first and foremost, her boy friend, to whom she prattled everything.

And so, rather than looking cagey, as all press agents did when talking with me, she simply looked unhappy. It upset her when she didn't have the real scoop on something. Sally took her gossip seriously. She was a Philadelphia girl, a Swarthmore English major who, thanks to a fortuitously answered want ad, had landed in show-business publicity. The job didn't pay much, but it had its fringe benefits—hyperexcited days and nights, a good table at Sardi's whenever she asked for it, and access to all the dirt on the Big Time Show Biz Personalities.

She was silent for a minute as she gave herself up to her hot-fudge sundae. Sally had a passion for sweets. She would be a fat lady someday. Right now, she was as slim, supple, and heedless as a greedy kitten. She rescued a dribble of whipped cream with the tip of her finger and licked it. At that moment, with her fresh face and modish mop of chestnut-brown curls, she looked about nine years old.

"Why didn't you like the movie?" she asked.

"I thought it was trite," I replied. "How many pictures have you seen where the young girl falls in love with the older married man?"

"But the man was a black militant. That's a different twist, isn't it?"

"The only thing black about that character was the casting. He talked white, thought white, and acted white. Even his clichés were white."

"Well, *we* think the movie will do very well," she maintained loyally.

"I think it will, too."

"Why, if you think it's so terrible?"

"Because of Penelope Wren. *She* makes the film exceptional."

"You like her, huh?"

"She's terrific. Real star quality. Beautiful, fascinating, a natural actress."

The press agent in Sally lit up happily. But then the woman in her had second thoughts. "Lucky you," she said, with a little jealous wrinkle of her nose. "To think you'll be doing a long, intimate piece on her!"

I laughed and took her hand. "I would never dare aspire so high. I know my place. I'm a mere ink-stained wretch. You're more my speed."

"You don't sound too happy about it."

"I'm *very* happy about it."

She smiled, the very gradual, contained smile she had when she was thinking a carnal thought. "Let's go back to your place," she said. Sweetly, she added, "You can pretend I'm Penelope Wren."

2 Penelope Wren, I was told, was very busy. She wouldn't be available for a lengthy interview until the following week. That was too long to wait. I got hold of her unlisted number and phoned her directly.

Penelope was politely cordial. In the movie, she had sounded folksy and mid-American. On the phone, her accent was upper class, devoid of flat *a*'s and *r*'s.

Yes, she *was* very busy that week. But they were having people over for drinks on Friday. Would I care to come? She wouldn't be able to talk to me for very long. But at least it would give me a chance to meet her husband and some of their friends.

Next, I called Hermann Dichter's office. I made an appointment to interview the director the next afternoon.

Thursday morning, a messenger from *View* arrived at my apartment with a bulging file. It contained all the published material on Penelope Wren and Elliot Karp.

The first clippings went back a long way, dating from James Wren's losing campaign for re-election to the U.S. Senate. They were newspaper write-ups depicting the candidate's private life. The accompanying photographs showed Wren with his happily smiling teen-age daughter. Glancing through these candidate-at-home pieces, I learned that Penelope's mother had died when the little girl was ten. Wren hadn't remarried. During her growing years, Penelope, an only child, had lived sometimes with her father, sometimes with her aunt.

There were some photographs of Penelope, taken when

she was a highly publicized model. I skipped over these to get to the Elliot Karp material.

The Karp clippings began with the front-page news article that had appeared at the time of his appointment to office. I studied his photograph. Karp had the squared-off features of a comic-strip hero. There was quite a lot of gray in his hair, an improbable gray when seen as the frame for such an unlined, boyish face. His smile was frank and winning, the kind of smile that tops an outthrust hand.

There were several more news articles, usually from the back pages of the *Times,* in which Karp announced a new policy for his agency or made a statement on an old policy. On the basis of this evidence, he seemed to be a fairly active municipal official. Or, at least, one who had a knack for finding his way into newsprint.

His official biography was at the rear of the file. This was the mimeographed release that the Mayor's press secretary had sent out. I noted down the main points.

Age: thirty-eight. Born in Buffalo. Father (deceased) was an insurance salesman. Education: Buffalo public schools and Syracuse University. B.A. in economics. Military service: naval intelligence. Rank at discharge: lieutenant. Past employment: sales manager for Telextron, Inc., Los Angeles, Calif.; executive with Prince and Lindley, the New York management-consultant firm. He had a two-year-old son, Elliot junior.

The profile of a fine young American, the kind of man my mother would have liked me to be.

The phone rang. It was Sally.

"It's all set," she said. "Monday at Sardi's. Twelve-thirty. Miss Wren has a very busy day. You'll have just two hours with her."

"Tell Miss Wren that I feel proud and privileged that she is granting me this audience."

"Don't be sarcastic."

"Then stop being such a great press agent. Be human for a moment."

"I don't have time to be human now, darling," she said apologetically. "I'm very rushed."

"Don't let me keep you."

"We'll see you at Sardi's, then," Sally said.

"We?"

"Yes, I'll be there."

"Honey," I said patiently, "you know I don't interview with a press agent around."

"I'll keep out of the way," Sally said brightly. "You won't even notice I'm there."

"I *will* notice. Press agents are painfully conspicuous. They are anxious and moist and kill all civilized conversation."

"I'm going to be there, darling." There was steel in her voice now. "Otherwise, there'll be no interview."

"Don't break my heart. *I* don't need the publicity."

"Well, then think of *me!* My boss says if I leave the two of you alone for even one minute he'll fire me."

That gave me pause. "He means that?"

"I don't know, but I don't want to test him. He's afraid you'll misquote."

"I *never* misquote."

"I know you don't, darling," she said quickly. "But some people *think* you do."

"I can see it now—this is going to be a great interview." I was starting to feel disgusted with the whole thing.

"Please, Don." The tough-chick press agent was gone. She was fragile and helpless and her voice was small with childlike appeal. "As a favor to me, be nice?"

"All right," I said, somewhat grudgingly, "it will be the way you want it. A nice, cozy threesome."

"I love you, darling."

"Now you tell me." I hung up.

I was annoyed. Sally, normally, was a warm and wonderful girl and most days of the week I thought I loved her. But at that moment I saw her simply as a press agent, and it was impossible to get any kind of interview with a press agent on top of you. Afterward, you were left with so little that, if you were to write at all, you would have to do a fabricated puff piece. I hadn't gotten where I was by writing puff pieces.

No, baby, I thought. Sorry, but I have my standards to maintain.

3 Hermann Dichter was engaged in his favorite sport— agent baiting. He could have kept me waiting until he was through, of course. But he had sent out word that I was to come in. Dichter had a touch of the Roman emperor to him: the larger the audience, the more satisfying the bloody spectacle.

Dichter was exactly centered behind a thirty-foot-long desk. His two assistants sat at one end, a slender shaggy-haired man of fifty and a slender shaggy-haired man of twenty-five. They were dressed identically in tailor-made, flunky, blue blazers, with gold buttons, and gray flannel slacks. At the other end, an agent sat with his client, an actor, an exploitable golden boy, with teased blond curls, clean sunburned neck, and capped teeth so bright white they made you want to squint. He had an eager-to-please but confused smile pasted on his face. The agent was an unhappy little man with a permanently squashed look to him. His collar was damp around his chubby neck.

Dichter motioned for me to take the chair opposite him. I sat.

"I am waiting," Dichter said to the agent.

"For what?" the agent asked uneasily.

"For you to say something intelligent." His voice, heavy with a German accent, rumbled out of him ponderously. "If you continue like this, I will think you are stupid. And you know I do not waste my time with stupid people."

The agent squirmed, but he had to endure it. His hatred for Dichter showed in his eyes. But the livelihoods of forty clients depended on his tact, his readily turned other cheek.

Hermann Dichter smiled with almost sensual affection. These exercises were pleasurable only when the victim couldn't fight back. That was what power was about, after all. To Dichter, this agent wasn't an unprepossessing, middle-aged man in a black suit. He was a luscious, naked maiden, bound hand and foot, chained to a pillar.

"All I'm asking is for you to be fair, Hermann," the agent said. "You can shoot around Jeff for a month. But if Jeff leaves the show now, without giving them time to find a replacement, it will create all kinds of bad feeling. Merrick will never use him again."

"So? If he leaves the show now, Merrick will never use him again. If he doesn't leave the show now, *I* won't use him. That is your choice."

"Hermann," the agent insisted, "there is a way of doing this so that everyone will be happy."

"You worry too much about making people happy, Marvin. You are too goodhearted to be an agent."

Dichter glanced at me, his eye twinkling, to make sure I appreciated this last sally. Then his gaze settled on the client, Jeff, who was looking steadily more confused and unhappy. "Are you satisfied with Marvin?" Dichter asked gently.

"Very satisfied," Jeff blurted out. "I owe him everything. He's been like a father to me."

"He was pushing two other clients for this role. You know that? *I* was the one who insisted on you."

"Now, wait a minute—!" Marvin protested.

"Let me tell you something, Jeff," Dichter said. "Take it from an old man who has been in this business forty years. An agent may or may not be a father. But an agent is not a humanitarian. He is not even ten percent of a humanitarian. Marvin is not worrying about you and Merrick. He is worrying about *himself* and Merrick. Take this role, Jeff." His voice dropped to a low, urgent tone, vibrant with concern for the young actor's well-being. "It is a good role. You will be terrific in it. It will change your life."

Jeff looked uncertainly at his agent. The actor's natural paranoid distrust of his managers was awake in his eyes. "Marvin, I—"

"Don't say anything!" his agent commanded. *"I'm* doing the negotiating."

"I'm taking this job, Marvin." Recklessly, he added, "To hell with Merrick!"

The discussion was ended. Jeff said a feverish round of good-byes and departed. Marvin went off with the older assistant to talk business.

I was left alone with Dichter and the young assistant. Dichter looked at me for a long moment and smiled. He smiled frequently, often pointlessly. It was as if he knew a smile was needed to temper his hobgoblin ugliness.

"So?" he said, at last. "You have come to apologize?"

"Apologize?" I echoed. "What for?"

"For the bad things you said about my last film."

The last time I had seen Dichter, we had been on a radio talk show together. I had said some fairly harsh things about the movie he was then pushing. There had been nothing remarkable about my comments, since almost every critic in the country had blasted the film.

"My God, Hermann, that was a year ago!"

He shrugged philosophically. "Ah, well, you have a right to your opinion. Idiotic though it is. I bear no grudges." He smiled magnanimously. "You will discover, if ever you get to know me better, that I have absolutely no ego."

It was something he obviously had said many times before. And yet I had the eerie feeling he really believed it.

"So? You want to ask me about my new film?"

"Not exactly."

The smile vanished from Dichter's face and he looked perplexed. He had a long memory for his bad notices, but he could be forgetful about the little, everyday things. Such as my reason for being there. The young assistant spoke up. "Mr. Skelton is writing an article on Penelope Wren."

"Ah, yes, of course. Burt," he said to his young assistant, "you can go do your work. I will take the very great risk of being alone with this dangerous man."

The young assistant departed.

"You want me to tell you about Penelope Wren?" Dichter asked. "She is a natural," he pronounced, in measured tones. "A fine actress and a wonderful, delightful person. She has style, refinement, sensitivity. She is, I think, the closest thing we have now to Grace Kelly." He paused, then added, "You may quote me."

I had my notebook open and I was making aimless squiggles across the page. "All right, Hermann. Now tell me what you *really* think of her."

Dichter folded his hands under his chin and gazed at me for a long, thoughtful moment. His tongue protruded from his mouth, withdrew, then protruded again, a rather repellent nervous tic. In that hairless head, the tongue seemed like some mollusk, thrusting out its moist head from a crevice in a tidal rock. "Off the record?" he asked, finally.

"Off the record."

"She is a monster."

"Would you care to elaborate?"

"Do not misunderstand me," he went on. "I do not say she is bad. She does all the very nice, good-girl things. But she is not a woman. When there is such a beautiful face, such a beautiful body, and there is no woman inside, then you have a monster."

"What makes you think she isn't a woman?"

"Let me tell you something, Don. With every woman, there

is a sexual thing. I have directed many actresses and this much I have learned. There is some sexual thing—always. She wants to be beaten, she wants to be adored, she wants her foot licked. It is one of these things, or something else, but if you look hard enough, you will find it. And I, the director, I am the biggest actor of all, you know? I must play the appropriate role. I must be the sexual thing that actress wants—so she will respond." His face darkened. "With Penelope, there is nothing."

"Maybe she's just plain healthy," I suggested.

He shook his head. "If a woman is healthy, there is a chemical change in her when a man is near. She is not the same as when another woman is near—or a dog or a chair. Penelope is the same always, as if there is no such thing as a man. She is charming. And she can seem very sexy, yes? But it is not real. It is click-click, like a machine."

"You would never guess it to see her in your movie."

"I told you, she is a fine actress."

"I understand you had a big blowup with Penelope."

Dichter gave a convincing rendition of injured surprise. "Who says that? People always say those things. They are not true! I get along *fabulously* with my actors."

"It isn't true you almost fired her?"

"Ah!" He let out his breath heavily. "You heard that, eh?"

"Is it true?"

He eyed me shrewdly. "If it were true, would I tell you?"

"You wouldn't have to tell me." I shrugged. "But then I'd just find out from someone else. I'd rather hear the unbiased version."

"Okay." He threw up his hands in a graceful what's-the-use-of-playing-games gesture. "Penelope was a very serious, very conscientious worker." He paused, then added meaningfully, "When she was there."

"She wasn't always there?"

"For two days she disappeared completely. No one knew

where she was. Her maid, her friends—they could tell us nothing. Her husband was in town. We tried him at his office, but we could never get through to him."

"When was this?"

Dichter thought hard. "It was a Tuesday and a Wednesday," he said slowly. "The second week of July."

"Did she have scenes to shoot on those days?"

"The most important scenes in the movie! Let me tell you, we went slightly crazy! Thursday, she was back. No explanation. No apology. She refused even to talk about it." His hobgoblin face purpled at the memory. "Yes, I lost my temper! Can you blame me?"

"And you almost fired her?"

"Ah, my God, how I wanted to! But it was out of the question," he said regretfully. "We were halfway through the shooting schedule."

"Have you met her husband, Elliot Karp?" I asked.

Dichter snorted with disgust. "Karp? He is another one like her. They deserve each other. The click-click plastic people." Dichter leaned forward. "Don, you are a scoundrel. But even you should be warned. You will like Penelope. She will charm you. You will think you understand her completely. In the end, you will understand nothing. You will have been played for a fool. You will have been taken in by a lie. A beautiful lie that walks in a beautiful body."

three

1 "Which are you?" the flaming-faced man asked. "Movie business or politics?"

"Is there nothing else?" I replied.

"Sometimes I wonder!" He laughed, a not altogether pleasant laugh. "At a guess, old boy, I wouldn't say you fall into either group."

"You've guessed right. And which are you?"

"Neither. I'm family." He held out his hand. "Tod Cushman. I'm Penelope's cousin."

"Don Skelton," I said, shaking his hand.

"Oh, yes. You're the chap who's writing the story on Penny."

"Penny?"

"Our childhood name for Penelope. Don't bother using it. No one calls her that any more."

He took a long, joyless swallow of his vodka. Tod Cushman was probably not much older than I was, but he gave a first impression of ravaged middle age. With his crimson cheeks, his venous nose, his slack mouth, he looked like some flaxen-haired rummy at the end of his rope. His accent, however, was very proper, very Grottlesex, an aristocratic drawl that sometimes slurred into a snarl.

"Is the Senator here?" I asked.

Cushman shook his head. "Uncle Jim doesn't get around much any more."

"Poor health?"

"You could say that."

"Oh, I'm sorry. I was hoping I could interview him. You think it's out of the question?"

"No, not actually," he said, after a moment. "Call him at his office."

"He still goes to his office?"

"Every day."

"I thought he was no longer active."

"He isn't. But he goes to his office." He took another swallow of the vodka and grimaced.

"What if I should want to talk with you?"

"Why would you want to talk with me? I thought you were writing about Penny as an actress."

"Her family life figures in it, too. Her childhood. I'm sure you have stories you could tell."

"Oh, yes. I have stories I could tell. But I don't know if I'd tell them to *you,* old boy."

I smiled, shrugged off the rebuff, and didn't pursue it further.

Suddenly Cushman's face distorted, a wince of distaste that came and went. He was looking past me. I turned.

Elliot Karp stood framed in the entrance arch of the living room, a beautifully trim man in a beautifully cut suit, with the aura of official limousine evanescing on him. He glanced around, faintly smiling, and took in his score of guests: the coiffed, pastel young ladies—his wife's social peers; the sharp-

faced, sporty, middle-aged men—the film people; the serious
younger men, who wore suits that were siblings to Karp's Ox-
ford-gray single-breasted—his subordinate bureaucrats.

Then he turned to one side and greeted two men who
were standing near the arch. These two looked distinctly out of
place in this smart crowd. They were nondescript types of about
Karp's age, blurred at the edges in their off-the-rack suits. Karp
punched the bigger one on the shoulder, and was punched in
return. Then he vigorously shook the hand of the other one,
gripping his arm gladly, as if he were seeing him for the first
time in a long while.

Penelope approached them. Karp, suddenly subdued, turned
to his wife. They kissed each other lightly on the lips.

They exchanged a few words, then both their heads turned
in my direction. Penelope left Karp and came toward me, smiling. The hem of her hostess gown rustled softly on the carpet as
she approached.

"I want you to meet Elliot," Penelope said, taking me by
the arm.

As we crossed the room, I asked, "When do I get a chance
to talk to *you?*"

"Some other time," she said. "In this house, Elliot is the
star. And I'm just a politician's wife. I smile nicely for the people and make sure there are enough sandwiches."

Karp and his friends were talking animatedly when we
joined them. Or, rather, the two other men were doing the talking, and Karp listened genially.

"You know what this clown did yesterday?" the larger one
said.

"No. What?" the other one responded. He was a little
fellow, politely eager, unstylish in his white socks and brown
loafers.

"He called my office. And he didn't tell the girl 'Elliot
Karp.' No, not Ellie. He told her 'Joe Namath.' How do you
like that? Joe Namath!"

"Jeez!" said the man in white socks, laughing.

"Was he this kind of clown when you knew him, Mike?"

"He was a clown, all right," Mike said.

Karp laughed good-naturedly. Penelope laughed, too, shortly, dutifully. Then she touched Karp's elbow. "Elliot, I'd like you to meet Don Skelton."

Karp turned to me. His face transformed into the serenely smiling face of his photographs. "How are you? Good to meet you." He shook my hand firmly.

It was a made smile, I noticed, a measured baring of teeth. The dark eyes stayed void. "I heard you're writing an article on Penelope," Karp said. "Do we get a look at the copy before you turn it in?"

"I'm afraid not," I replied. "It just isn't done."

"That's all right. I understand." His soft voice was warm and, against all logic, he sounded totally sympathetic. And yet I detected a sense of discomfort; very slight, about as much as there would have been if his collar were too snug or his shoes pinched. I didn't know whether it was something that was always there or whether he already suspected the purpose of my piece. "Is this article Blake Hivnor's idea?" Karp asked.

"Yes. He thinks a major piece is due on Penelope. She's going to be a smash in her film."

"Oh, I don't think so," Penelope murmured.

Karp's smile was half pleased, half pained. "I'll have to get used to that, I guess. Being married to a movie star."

"Maybe *you* should be in a movie, Ellie," the big man said.

Karp seemed astonished by the idea. "What would a klutz like me do in front of a camera? I'll leave the acting to Penelope."

"Then you better watch out," his friend persisted. "She'll end up more famous than you."

"I don't want fame," Karp said. "I can live without it.

All the reward I need is the satisfaction I feel when I help an operation work more smoothly." It was a modest, earnest statement of the executive's credo. It didn't sound terribly convincing.

"Don," Karp said, belatedly making the introductions, "this is Lionel Stern—and this is Mike Hamowy."

"I'm an old friend of Ellie's from back home," Mike Hamowy blurted out.

"Buffalo?" I inquired.

"That's right! Buffalo." Mike seeemd delighted that I was aware of the existence of his native city. "I'm in town for a few days. So I looked up Ellie. We haven't seen each other in—" He looked at Karp. "Jeez, how long is it?"

"Too long," Karp said. He turned to Penelope. "Have you and Mike had a chance to talk?"

"Only for a moment," she said, "when he came in."

"He was my best friend," Karp said.

"Oh, yes." She gazed at Mike thoughtfully. "Excuse me," she murmured. "I have to go check the ice." She moved off toward the kitchen.

There was a brief silence. "Tell me, Mike," Lionel Stern asked suddenly, "was this clown as big an operator when he was a kid?" Lionel was Karp's toady, I gathered; but he was the kind of toady who fawns with insults.

"If you really want to know," Mike replied, "he was kind of quiet."

"Studious?" I asked.

"No. No more than the rest of us, anyway." Quickly, he added, "But he's smart."

"Sure Ellie's smart!" Lionel said heartily. "It takes brains to be able to read the stock prices in Yiddish."

Karp laughed, taking the ribbing like a good sport. But his eyes were uneasy.

A beeper started beeping. The high-pitched, urgent signal

seemed to come from Karp's chest. He reached into his inside pocket. The beeping stopped. "See you later," he said. "I've got a call." He walked away and disappeared into the next room.

The remote-control magic of the beeper had left Mike Hamowy profoundly impressed. "Jeez, was that the Mayor, you think?"

"Maybe," Lionel said. "Or it could be one of Ellie's broads."

"I don't see how you can talk to Ellie the way you do," Mike said mildly, but with genuine distress. "He's a big public official, after all."

"Aw, Ellie knows I love him," Lionel said, dismissing the rebuke with a wave of his hand. "For Christ's sake, I was Ellie's friend when he was peddling chewing gum!"

"Peddling chewing gum?" Mike echoed confusedly. "I thought he was with that big firm—what was it called?"

"Prince and Lindley," I offered.

"You want to know how he got that job?" Lionel was addressing me now, not Mike.

"I assume his father-in-law had something to do with it," I said.

"The Senator set up the appointment, yeah. With old man Prince, himself. But it was Ellie who *got* the job. You want to know how he did it?" Lionel glanced around, then, lowering his voice slightly, went on. "Ellie went to the library and looked up Prince's speeches—all his statements—all the articles he'd written. He memorized them. Then, when he went to see him, Ellie just sat there and spouted all of Prince's ideas—even using the old man's own words. Of course, Prince thought he was a goddamned genius. The most brilliant young guy he'd ever met!" He laughed, then shook his head with grudging admiration. "What an operator!"

Mike wasn't smiling. "See you," he said. He walked away, rather abruptly.

Mike went over to the buffet spread and studied it. After a

few moments, I joined him. "He really shouldn't talk that way," Mike said. He ran a fingertip along the edge of a piece of bread. "Stale. We wouldn't serve bread this old at our restaurant."

"You own a restaurant in Buffalo?"

"My family owns it. I run it." Rejecting the idea of a sandwich, he put some cheese dip on a cracker, instead. He wandered over to a corner, and I followed.

"How long has it been since you last saw Elliot?" I asked.

"Well, I talked with him on the phone once when he came up to see his mom. But actually saw him?" He thought. "Seventeen years." Mike brooded silently for a moment. Then, half to himself, he said, "God, I feel like an idiot! Maybe he doesn't even remember."

"Remember what?"

"Our pact."

"You made a pact?"

"Yeah. We swore that, no matter where we were or what we were doing, we'd see each other again in twenty years. On a particular day." He shrugged unhappily. "Today is the day."

It was a common enough pubescent ritual, but quick arithmetic told me that Ellie and Mike had been well beyond the age for that kind of thing. "How old were you?" I asked. "About eighteen?"

He nodded. "Eighteen." As if he had read my thought, he added, "Almost grown men." His smile was a bit sheepish. "I know, it seems silly. But the circumstances were special. You see, I'd just saved Ellie's life."

"How did that happen?"

"We were swimming in a lake. A guy driving a speedboat didn't see Ellie. Hit him and broke his back. The son of a bitch didn't even stop. He went zooming off and left me there with Ellie. I kept him afloat for half an hour until help came.

"He was in the hospital for months," he went on. "One time, when I was visiting him there, he got to talking about how grateful he felt, what a good friend I was. So we made this pact.

We were to meet again in twenty years. Twenty years from the day I saved his life." He grimaced slightly, as if the sentimentality of it embarrassed him now. "We never mentioned it again. I forgot about it. But then, when I began reading about him in the papers, I remembered. I didn't know whether *he* remembered—but I didn't want to fail him. So I came down here, called him, and—" His voice trailed off.

"You should have reminded him just now. Casually."

"What's the use? He's changed. He's not the same guy." He paused, then added, "To tell you the truth, he's never really been the same since that accident."

"How was he different after the accident?"

"Well, for one thing, Ellie was an athlete. Nothing great— but pretty good. He was a starting halfback on our high-school team. And he had hopes of getting an athletic scholarship to some college. All that was over, of course, when his back got screwed up. And it changed other things, too. For instance, it kept him from going into the service. That made a big difference when he—"

"Wait a minute," I cut in. "He was never in the service?"

"No. Like I said, his back kept him out. He tried to enlist in the Navy, but they turned him down."

"When did he try to enlist?"

"When he dropped out of college."

"He dropped out?"

"Or flunked out. I never knew which."

"What did he do then?"

"He hung around home for about a year. Worked in our restaurant as the night manager. Then he disappeared."

Mike had answered these last few questions rather impatiently, as one does when asked about irrelevant things, barely glancing at me as he tossed off his replies. But now he took in my expression and gave me a quizzical look. "Something wrong?" he asked.

"I'm surprised, that's all. Ellie tells a different story these days."

"He does?" He shrugged. "Ellie always liked to embellish."

Elliot Karp was returning. He paused to shake hands with a deferential, eagerly smiling man. Then he came on toward us. "That was one of the Mayor's aides on the phone," he explained as he rejoined us. "They just don't give me a moment."

"I can imagine," Mike said.

Karp regarded Mike warmly. "We've got a lot of catching up to do."

"We sure do," Mike agreed.

"You're married now, huh?"

"Yeah. Dorothy and I have been married for nine years." Karp thought. "Dorothy Warshaw?"

"No. Another Dorothy. One you don't know."

"Got any kids?"

"Two. A boy and a girl."

"That's terrific," Karp said. He beamed at Mike with genuine enough pleasure. But his kindliness seemed somewhat conferred, slightly patronizing, as if he were a congressman talking to a constituent.

Mike was gazing up into his face hopefully, as if he were searching for some sign. "Ellie," he asked, "do you know what day this is?"

Karp looked at him uncomprehendingly. And, in that moment, I saw the hope drain from Mike's expression.

The beeper started beeping again. "There it goes," Karp said, with a rueful shrug. "You guys will have to excuse me. It's the way it is these days. We've got a tough campaign ahead." He gave Mike a friendly tap on the shoulder. "We'll talk some more later."

"I've got to go," Mike said. His voice was dispirited.

"Already?"

"I've got an appointment."

"Well, call me again," Karp said. "Next time you're in town."

"I will," Mike said.

Karp walked away briskly, swiftly weaving his way through the guests. Mike watched him until he went out of sight.

2 My lunch date with Penelope was for twelve-thirty. I went uptown at noon. This gave me time to search out Sally's car.

It wasn't hard to find. It was a very recognizable red Volvo and it was parked on West Forty-sixth Street, half a block from the building that housed Sally's P.R. firm. As I expected, the car was parked illegally. The rear end was poked into a no-parking zone.

Sally had had her driver's license only six months, and already the parking tickets were piling up. It was useless for me to tell her she'd be better off taking taxis. She was enamored of the Volvo, her first car.

I went into a phone booth and dialed Tommy Anthony's number. There were six rings and then a befogged "Hello?"

"For Christ's sake," I snapped, "you're not still asleep, are you?"

"No, man. Honest!" Tommy said quickly, unconvincingly. "I been up an hour."

I didn't pursue it. Tommy, I knew, lived a highly disorganized life. He was an actor and a member of the hard-core unemployed. He kept himself going with odd jobs. He was, at various times, a pallbearer, a toy demonstrator at Macy's, and a Nedick's fink—one of those undercover types who go from shop to shop, nibbling hot dogs and checking up on the waitresses. I sometimes called on him for mildly clandestine tasks.

"Everything is set," I said. "We go ahead according to plan."

"I dig."

I told him where Sally's car was parked, gave him some final instructions, and hung up.

It was a five-minute walk to Sardi's. I arrived there at exactly twelve-thirty.

The restaurant was moderately full. Nearly all the banquette places along the walls, beneath the caricature drawings of the greats and near-greats of the stage, were occupied, mostly by actorish young men and women with uplifted profiles.

Penelope and Sally were at an interior table, one of the front-and-center tables reserved for very special people. They looked up as I approached and both smiled simultaneously. Sally, I noticed, was wearing the dress I had told her was my favorite, an orange-and-yellow print that clung to her figure. Penelope was wearing a rather severe white pants suit. Even so, the eye naturally went to Penelope.

"What kind of star are you?" I asked Penelope, as I sat. "Don't you know that *you're* the one who's supposed to keep *me* waiting?"

"I haven't been a star for that long," she replied. "I find it hard to be rude."

"You'll learn."

A waiter appeared, bringing two Bloody Marys for the ladies. I asked for a martini on the rocks, glanced at the menu, and ordered a house specialty, cannelloni.

The three of us looked at each other in a moment of mute self-consciousness. Sally, as was her duty, broke the ice. "Well, at last you meet," she said brightly.

"We've met already," Penelope said.

"You have?"

"We had Don over to our place for drinks on Friday."

"Oh," Sally said uneasily.

"But we didn't really get a chance to talk to each other," Penelope added.

"This will be our first real conversation," I assured Sally.

This seemed to make Sally feel a little better. "Well, then, you're already acquainted," she said cheerily. "You should feel more at home with each other now."

"I still feel rather inhibited," Penelope said. She looked at me and quickly added, "About the interview, I mean." She smiled, a charmingly self-deprecating smile. "I know I'm supposed to say all kinds of witty, printable things. But I'm afraid I may come across like an absolute dunce."

"This surely isn't your first interview?" I murmured, politely skeptical.

"No. I've had a few recently. The other day, I was on one of these TV interview programs—I don't remember the name. Every time there was a commercial break, the host would ask me, 'Do you have any anecdotes?' " She laughed. "All I could think of were some dirty stories we used to tell each other in boarding school."

"Did you tell one?"

"Almost. But I thought better of it."

"Well, you don't need any prepared anecdotes with me," I said, taking out my notebook. "I'll just ask you some questions. Answer them any way you want."

She nodded. "All right. What's the first question?"

"We'll start with something easy. When did you first know you wanted to be an actress?"

"I don't know that even now. I mean, I love acting. But I'm not sure I want to make a lifetime career out of it. The career is something that's just—" she shrugged helplessly— *"happened."*

"But it wasn't a total accident," I pointed out. "You took acting classes, you worked in summer theater—"

"That was before I married Elliot."

"Being married to Elliot has changed everything?"

"Completely. Now I put my marriage first. Of course, if I'm offered a movie, and it doesn't interfere with my family, I'll do it. On the other hand, if Elliot, for some reason, should have to move to Washington—" she paused to make sure I caught the significance, the intimation of pending glory—"I would want to be with him at all times."

It was a textbook answer to a textbook question. I kept it on that same banal level, asking the tritest questions I knew—what did she think of the new sexual freedom in movies?, and so on. She answered each one flawlessly, without missing a beat. I asked her about her own movie. "It makes a very important statement, I think," she said. Hermann Dichter? "A genius. I learned *so* much from him." It turned out she *did* have some prepared anecdotes. Without much prompting, she came forth with a couple—of the Funny Things That Happened on Location variety.

Sally was beaming. She erupted into little trills of laughter every time her client said something that faintly smacked of wit. Occasionally, she interjected a supportive phrase—"Oh, yes!" "Tell him about that, Penelope." "Fantastic!"

As the interview went on, Penelope started to look restive, almost anxious. She may not have had much experience as a movie star, but she had been raised as a politician's daughter and she knew what made good copy. She sensed the flatness of what she was saying. In politics or in show business, it was a losing pitch.

I was biding my time. Two o'clock came. In spite of myself, I turned my head to glance at the maître d'. He was regarding the diners with his usual bemused half smile. Beside him on the wall, the phone stayed silent.

I began to get worried. But I kept asking questions, kept noting down answers, and waited.

At five minutes past the hour, a captain came up to our table and placed a telephone in front of Sally. "For you, Miss Fry," he said. "Someone from your office." He plugged in the phone and left.

Sally picked up the receiver. "Hello?— The red Volvo? Yes, that's my car— *What?*" Her eyes widened with shock.

"But they can't do that! Tell them to stop doing that!" There was a longish pause. Tommy Anthony was padding his part a little. "Yes, yes, I'll be right over!" Sally hung up. There was a look of horror in her eyes. "They're about to tow away my car!"

She didn't delay a second. Her reaction was something visceral, pure mother instinct. She rose and dashed out of the restaurant.

I put away my notebook and pencil. "Poor kid, I feel for her," I murmured sympathetically. "That little Volvo is her baby."

The waiter served our coffee. Penelope sat back, visibly relaxing. She took out a vial of noncaloric sweetener and let a drop fall into her cup. As she raised the cup to her lips, her large blue eyes held on me, appraising me. Finally, she commented, "You're not so frightening."

"Were you expecting a monster?"

"No. But I was warned about you."

"Sally put in a good word for me, huh?"

"She didn't say anything. I knew about you already."

"I wasn't sure you'd read my stuff."

"I haven't. But my friends have told me about you."

"What do they say?"

"That you like to hurt people in print."

"I don't like it," I said, "nor do I dislike it. I'm an honest reporter. I write the truth. Some people find the truth painful."

"Is it really necessary that everyone know the truth?"

"People, as a rule, would rather hear the truth about public figures than the usual lies."

"I wonder," she murmured.

"Anyway," I asked, "why should *you* worry? Do you think you've said anything so far that would compromise you?"

She smiled slightly. "Hardly. In fact, I still can't understand why Blake wants an article on me at all."

I picked up on her use of Hivnor's first name. "You know Blake Hivnor personally?"

"Of course. Elliot and I used to see a lot of the Hivnors. Margrit and I were good friends."

"Margrit," I repeated. I vaguely remembered that Hivnor had been married to a Swedish beauty, a model of some renown. "That's Blake's ex-wife?"

"They're still married, as far as I know. Separated. Margrit hasn't bothered getting a divorce."

"Do you still see them?"

"No, neither of them," she said tersely. "We grew apart." Her quick, hard look warned me not to pursue the matter further.

I felt suddenly uneasy. I, of course, hadn't suspected this personal connection between my editor and my subject. Penelope's tone had implied that the connection had been a good deal more than casual, the termination of it something less than friendly. It gave a quite different complexion to my assignment. It occurred to me now that Blake might be playing some very different game within our game.

"Well, then," I said, "if Blake knows you, he has a special interest in your career."

"Perhaps," she said.

I stared at my notes for a moment and tried to figure it out. I had assumed that Elliot Karp was an incidental target, and that Blake, for some hidden, power-drive reason, was after the Mayor. It was a matter of political warfare, I had thought, and it wasn't for me, as an honest mercenary, to question it. But now I had the strong sense that I had unwittingly let myself get involved in some twisted personal matter. And I didn't like the idea at all.

"Shall we continue with the interview?" Penelope suggested coolly.

I focused again on the business at hand. "How did you first meet Elliot?"

"I met him on the Cape. In Dennis. I was touring with a summer package—*Philadelphia Story*. One night, when we were eating dinner at the inn, I noticed this absolutely gorgeous man sitting by himself at a table. He kept watching me. You get used to people staring at you in public places when you're playing small towns. But this was different," she said, with a smile. "He happened to go to the play that night. Later, Elliot said he was surprised to see me up on that stage. He had thought I was one of the socialites who had summer places there—not just a hired mountebank."

"Why was Elliot up there? Was he on vacation?"

She hesitated for just an instant. "Yes," she replied. "After the show," she went on, "Elliot came backstage to see me. He told me how much he liked my performance. He seemed very gentle, very kind. He asked me out for a drink." With a graceful little gesture, she concluded, "And that's how it started. For the rest of that summer, he followed me around."

"On the tour? He wasn't tied down by a job?"

She didn't answer the question directly. "He was free to move around," she said.

I jotted down a question mark after the reply, then went on. "Does Elliot approve of your being a—hired mountebank?"

"Oh, of course. He's been tremendously supportive."

"What about when you were making the movie? Was there any friction between you?"

She wrinkled her brow, as if the question baffled her. "Between Elliot and me? Why do you ask that?"

"Dichter mentioned that you'd disappeared for a couple of days during shooting. He didn't know the reason. He said you never told him. I was wondering if there might have been some trouble at home."

Penelope stared at me for a long, silent moment, her eyes mesmeric and unreadable. She had the film star's trick of using a rapt, luminous gaze as a barrier. "If I didn't tell Hermann," she said, at length, "it was because I thought it was none of his business." Her frosty tone implied that it was none of mine, either. "But I don't want you to be under the impression that Elliot was the reason. He had nothing to do with it." She paused, then went on, "My father had a heart attack. Not a serious one—but there's always danger. I spent those two days by his side."

"Why make such a secret of it? I mean, a mild heart attack isn't something that most people try to hide."

"You'd have to live in a politician's family to understand. You see, my father has his enemies. Poor health is something that can be used against a man."

She said this with earnestness, as if the answer made perfect sense. In fact, it didn't. "But he has no plans for running for office now, has he?" I asked.

"No. But my father isn't completely out of the political picture. He never will be, as long as there's a chance his party might need him." With appeal in her look, she said, "I'd appreciate it if you'd keep what I've told you a secret."

"If you wish. I'm not writing this piece on your father, anyway."

"Thank you, Don." Her smile was suddenly warm and grateful. There was an intimacy to it. It implied that this shared confidence had brought us closer. I was almost one of the family now.

But, in fact, all communication had ended. When I tried to continue the questioning, Penelope abruptly changed the subject. She made it quite clear that the interview was over. Through the next few minutes, as we downed our cooling coffee, we occupied ourselves with small talk, the weary small talk of two people at the end of a lunch that has gone on too long.

I was almost glad when Sally reappeared. I didn't see her come back in. But I happened to look up and there she was, standing by our table, a little breathless from running, glaring at me.

"How's the little heap?" I asked her.

"Just fine," Sally muttered. She looked at Penelope, then looked at me, but said nothing. She had too much press agent's poise to show her anger. And too much good sense to mention the trick I had played on her. "Well, what have I missed?" she asked, as she sat.

"Your coffee," Penelope said, indicating the cold, untouched cup at Sally's place. "Excuse me," she said. She rose and headed toward the powder room.

Sally waited until Penelope was out of sight. "All right, you sneaky bastard," she hissed furiously, "what did she say?"

I shrugged. "More platitudes. Dullest interview I've had in ages."

"You wouldn't have gone to all that trouble to get rid of me if you weren't after something." Insistently, anxiously, she asked, "What did you get?"

"I did it for the principle of the thing, baby. Don't worry," I reassured her, "it will be a nice, upbeat piece."

3   "The Greeks," Tod Cushman said, fondly patting the small stack of leather-bound books on the side table by his chair. "The Greeks can be a great comfort, old boy." He picked up the top volume, opened it to where a place was marked, and, reading from the page, intoned a few lines of mellifluous Greek.

"I'm sorry," I said. "I don't know Greek."

"Didn't think you did." Cushman studied the passage for a moment. " 'Some Thracian has my shield,' " he recited, translating now. " 'Being somewhat in a hurry, I left it in a bush. Well, never mind, I saved my neck. And I'll get me another one just as good.' Archilochus. Seventh century B.C."

His hands, as they held the book, were still shaking slightly. But his face was no longer a waxen yellow. The blood was coursing and his cheeks were flaring up to their usual startling shade of red.

I had made the mistake of arriving at his apartment early, a few minutes before three rather than a quarter past. Three in the afternoon, it seemed, was Cushman's strict starting time for his day of drinking. I had caught him sweating and unready. But now, ten minutes and two vodkas later, he was almost his normal self.

"Is classical studies your field?" I asked.

He closed the book and put it aside. "Not professionally," he said. "Publishing is my racket. It used to be, anyway."

"Which house were you with?"

"Several of them. No point in mentioning any one— they're all the same. Schlockmeisters!" he spat out. "Peddlers of masturbational fantasies for frecklebellies. No, there's no place for me in that business. A hundred years ago, maybe. I would have enjoyed nursing old Henry James along. But now—" He went silent for a moment as he sourly contemplated his dead career. "I don't miss that world. And it doesn't miss me." With a short laugh, he concluded, "So I sit here and read Greek."

The sunlight slanted through the tall windows of the study, casting a crosshatched pattern on the books that lined the far wall. These books were, for the most part, in sets, with fine morocco and calf bindings. It was clearly an inherited library, the kind that can't be collected nowadays. In fact, everything in that room seemed to have been passed down from some other time; the furniture, the prints that depicted country scenes. Even Cushman's red velvet smoking jacket was of the style that might have been worn by that other, turn-of-the-century Cushman who had pieced together this scholar's haven.

"I was surprised when you called, Mr. Cushman," I said. "The first time we spoke, I got the impression you didn't want to be interviewed."

"I have reconsidered," he said.

"Why?"

Cushman didn't answer. Instead, he asked, "How do Elliot and Penny strike you? Their life together?"

"They seem to have an ideal marriage."

"An ideal marriage," he repeated thoughtfully. "How would you define that, old boy? The union of two very discreet people?"

"That's one way of looking at it."

"Yes, they're discreet," he said. "Everyone in our family has always been discreet. Our drunks get retired to the country. Our philanderers get sent abroad. Our homosexuals get married off. And when someone makes an unwise choice of a mate," he went on, more pointedly, "there's not one of us who'll speak a word of criticism. Not outside the family fold, anyway." His mouth twisted bitterly. "Well, I'm tired of being discreet. Discretion is a bore. And it might be useful to bring *some* things out into the open." He took a swallow of his vodka, then asked, "So, tell me, what's the picture you get so far of this—ideal marriage?"

"A great romance. They fell in love at first sight, their marriage has been blissful—and, for all I know, they'll live happily ever after."

Cushman looked slightly sick. I didn't know whether it was the vodka in his stomach or my statement. "I didn't realize you were such a sentimentalist, Skelton," he said. "There *was* a great romance. But it wasn't between Penny and Elliot."

I waited for him to go on. When he didn't, I cued him. "Penny and someone else?"

He nodded. "I can't tell you his name. He's rather famous in his line of work—which is acting. He happens to be married. Not that Penny couldn't have broken up that marriage easily enough. The chap was gaga over her. But it never got that far.

Uncle Jim—the Senator—saw to that. He put the old paternal foot down."

"He didn't like the man?"

"He never met him. Uncle Jim didn't like the idea of a messy and very public scandal. We're not finicky in our family, old boy. Adultery can be quite all right. Loads of fun, in fact." He raised his finger in mock sternness. "But it must never—*never*—get into print."

"Where does Elliot fit in?" I asked.

"He was the young man on the make who was there at exactly the right time to catch Penny on the rebound."

"Maybe she would have been attracted to him, anyway, rebound or not."

"Attracted, yes. Penny had her flings—and he was good enough for a three-day affair, I suppose. But marriage?" Cushman looked incredulous. "To a nobody who'd wandered by peddling dental gum?"

"What's this about dental gum?" I asked perplexedly.

"That's what Elliot was doing when Penny met him. He was a drummer, working the New England territory. Some charlatan had invented a chewing gum that was supposed to act as a dentifrice. Leave your teeth so white they'd gleam in the dark." He laughed. "I tried it. It didn't work."

"And Karp was peddling this product?"

"From drugstore to drugstore. And getting nowhere."

"Then I don't get it," I said. "The Senator stopped one romance. Why did he let Penelope marry Elliot?"

"He didn't just *let* her. He kicked up quite a fuss, in fact. But it wasn't the same thing. With the other fellow, Penny was breaching one of the Commandments. That made it a family concern. With Elliot, she was simply breaching good taste. She was of the age of consent and there was nothing anyone could do." He paused thoughtfully. "Yes," he went on, "Elliot came along at just the right time. He was the perfect combination—a

Jew with no background, no money, and no prospects. Exactly what Penny needed to get back at Uncle Jim."

"You're not trying to tell me that she married Karp just to spite her father?"

"It isn't the only time that's ever happened, old boy."

"Well, then, all things considered, Karp has worked out pretty well, hasn't he? I mean, for a Jew with no background?" I said, acidly echoing the ethnic slur.

"Good God, Skelton, give me some credit!" Cushman said disgustedly. "This has nothing to do with Elliot's being a Jew. There is no smarter man than a smart Jew. Even a bigot like myself—" he smiled disarmingly—"has great respect for the smart Jew. But Elliot is a *dumb* Jew. And there's not much to be said for a dumb Jew, is there, old boy?"

I felt a sudden distaste for this man. But I controlled myself, kept my tone reasonable as I pointed out, "The Mayor must have seen something in him. He made him Director of the Agency for Urban Development."

"What the Mayor saw was James Wren's son-in-law, nothing more. As for his job—well, I imagine the amount of ability you need to cut the mustard in one of those cushy political appointments is about as much as it takes to get in and out of a limousine without falling on your face."

"You exaggerate," I murmured.

"Not when it comes to Elliot," he said emphatically. "I *know* the man. Everything he touches turns to dross. When they were first married, he took all of Penny's money and lost it in some cockeyed stock speculation. He bought two thousand shares in a firm that manufactured some kind of fruit squeezer, or something ridiculous like that. When the stock hit bottom, Elliot was so deep in debt he even had to come to *me* to borrow money."

"Bad luck," I said.

"Stupid greed," he countered. A perplexed, disturbed look came onto his face. "But he seems to have some kind of hold over Uncle Jim. He has him completely bamboozled. Uncle Jim has helped Elliot every step of the way—made everything possible. And he didn't *have* to do it." He shook his head wonderingly. "To hear Uncle Jim tell it, Elliot is brilliant, selfless, hard-working, honest, a natural leader of men."

"You have to respect the Senator's opinion," I said. "He's spent a lifetime judging character."

"He's not the man he once was," he said.

"In what way is he different?"

Cushman just stared at me, an icy stare that told me I was being presumptuous. "Senator Wren isn't your story."

"Elliot Karp isn't, either. I'm doing my story on Penelope."

"Elliot is part of her story." He leaned forward. "Find out about him! Find out the whole stinking truth about him! Before it's too late—for Penny, for Uncle Jim, for all of us."

4 It was one of the older, smaller office buildings in the Wall Street area. In its time, it had been an elegant palace for merchant princes. But now it stood, its iron ornamentation rusted, moldering in the shadow cast by a new skyscraper.

As I walked along the sixth-floor corridor, checking out the names on the frosted glass of the doors, I got mainly a sense of baffled hopes and transience. The single room of a travel agency was dark. After that, there was an accountant, then someone in the diamond business, then someone who was in unspecified export-import.

At the very end of the corridor, I found the office I was looking for. I knocked. There was no response. I knocked again and waited through a minute of continuing silence. Then I opened the door part way and peeked in.

Senator Wren was behind his desk, sitting quite straight, his eyes wide and unblinking. He seemed to be in a trance.

I stepped in and, very quietly, closed the door after me. The Senator's eyes didn't flicker. Nothing about him acknowledged my presence. He was formally dressed, in a dark suit and vest, with the three crisp points of a handkerchief jutting up from his breast pocket. He seemed rather like a diplomat who was attentively hearing out a long-winded head of state; there was a faint, bemused smile on his lips.

His smile widened. Only then did it occur to me that he was gazing at some particular thing.

I turned my head and looked. A Sony TV set rested on a small stand. On the tiny screen, a silver-shirted cowboy was throwing long, telegraphed punches at an outlaw type in a black shirt. The sound was off and, without the deceitful sound effects of *crack* and *splot,* the fight seemed even phonier than usual. It was quite apparent that each punch was missing by a good six inches.

The black-shirted heavy went down for the last time. The commercial came on. "Problem solved," Senator Wren said.

The sound of his voice startled me. I had half convinced myself that, for some reason, I was invisible to him. But now, when I looked at him again, he was regarding me pleasantly, with a genial smile. "You can turn off the set," he said.

I did so. "I like to see a problem cleanly settled," Wren said. "Nowadays, you see some black fellow in a black hat kicking the bejesus out of a white man in a white hat. Or you see nice Indians being massacred by an addlebrained Custer. It may be liberal, but it's confusing." He gestured to a chair in front of the desk. "Sit down."

I went to the chair and sat. "I hope I'm not interrupting you," I said, indicating the sheet of paper in the typewriter.

"Just catching up on some correspondence."

At one corner of his desk, there was a large stack of unfolded letters. They looked rather stale and bent at the edges. At the other corner, three sealed envelopes, stamped and addressed, overlapped one another. A pile of letter stationery was near me. I took a quick upside-down look and was surprised to see that the stationery was emblazoned with the words "Wren and Sons."

Wren and Sons no longer existed. This once-distinguished investment firm had been one of the most notable casualties of the 1969–1970 recession. It had teetered on the verge of a scandalous bankruptcy, but somehow had managed to expire gracefully. Few of the customers were seriously hurt and the only real damage was to James Wren's reputation as a money manager.

Wren, grandson of the founder, had taken on the presidency of the firm only after he had failed to be re-elected to the U.S. Senate. His firm's ignominious demise, as much as anything else, had postponed his comeback in politics. So it seemed peculiar, to say the least, that he would have a reminder of this debacle at the top of each letter that he wrote.

"As I said on the phone, Senator," I began, "I'm writing a piece on your daughter. I'm very appreciative of your giving me some of your time to talk about her."

"It's my pleasure," Wren said. "I happen to be a doting father. I take more pride in Penelope's accomplishments than in my own."

"Have you seen her movie?"

"Of course. I think it's a fine film. And Penelope is absolutely wonderful in it."

"How do you feel about the story it tells? The love affair between the black man and the upper-class white girl?"

He wrinkled his brow briefly. "What do you mean, how do I feel? There has been a certain amount of progress in this area, after all. And people of different races do sometimes fall in love, I believe."

"What about the love scenes? Weren't you concerned at all about what your friends might think? Your associates?"

These were testing questions. Wren, during his twelve years in the Senate, had fought for civil rights and fair housing. But, as I knew, the private aristocrat could sometimes be different from the public man.

"The movie tells a fictional story," Wren reminded me patiently. "And my daughter is a professional actress. My daughter and I never confuse fiction with reality."

I lit a cigarette unhurriedly, giving myself time to plan a new line of questioning. All the while, Wren regarded me calmly, displaying neither interest nor boredom. He had faced the press a thousand times in his life and he had it down pat, the trick of seeming open and available while remaining totally uninvolved. Even so, his remoteness had something odd about it. His benign expression was as fixed as if it had been set in wax. In fact, that was the image that came to my mind as I looked at him—a handsome, silver-haired mannequin in a display window, a semblance after the fact.

"Does Harry Thurston know you're writing this?" Wren asked.

I stared at him uncomprehendingly. The question had come out of nowhere; it didn't seem to make sense. "What does Harry Thurston have to do with it?"

"He owns you."

"I beg your pardon?"

"Your magazine. The one you write for." He took in my surprised reaction. "You didn't know?"

"I've been away," I admitted.

"He bought it last month."

I had heard the rumors before I had gone into my winter's hibernation. At the time, however, they had been discounted. Harry Thurston was the biggest builder and developer in the East. But his conglomerate had not previously shown any interest in publishing ventures.

"You don't approve of Thurston?" I ventured.

"Hardly," Wren said. "It was his money that beat me. And his money is going to try to beat the Mayor in November."

I maintained my mild smile. But underneath I was quite shaken. It had been bad enough when I had discovered that the target of my piece was a former personal friend of my editor. It would be far worse if it turned out that I was really doing the bidding of an unprincipled publisher, one of the greediest old reactionaries in the country.

"I warned Penelope about this article of yours," Wren said. "But she feels it's her duty to co-operate in publicizing the movie. She's a very responsible girl."

"I assure you, Senator," I said, "I didn't know about Harry Thurston until you told me just now."

"I believe you. I've never had reason to doubt the ignorance of journalists," he said dryly. "Anyway," he went on, with a smile, "show business is a long way from politics, isn't it?"

"Not in Penelope's case." I put aside all disturbing thoughts and went back to work. "After all, she's still in the world of politics as Elliot Karp's wife. For instance, won't she be campaigning for the Mayor? In the primary? And in the November election?"

"Yes, I believe she intends to. But Elliot will be doing most of that. He's a forceful speaker and he has a good appearance—very effective on TV. The Mayor could use five more like him. He needs all the help he can get this year."

"You're proud of your son-in-law, aren't you, Senator?"

"Very proud."

"That's generous of you."

He frowned. "What's so generous about it?"

"Well, sometimes a father gets a little jealous of his daughter's love for another man."

"That's crap," Wren said. "My daughter loves her husband, as well she should. But the love that Penelope and I have for each other is special. Very special." With a thin, meaningful smile, he added, "Elliot is no threat to it."

I detected an undertone in these last words, a hint of

something that was not friendly to Elliot. Emboldened, I proceeded into the more risky area. "Your son-in-law is from a very different background," I said. "Weren't there family objections to the marriage?"

"Some of the relatives were not exactly delighted by the prospect of their union."

"But it had *your* approval?"

"Not completely. Not at the outset, anyway. I thought they were acting too hastily. I felt they should have taken more time to consider their decision."

"It was a short engagement?"

"It was hardly an engagement at all. They met in July. They were married in October." He was silent for a moment, then he smiled; it was a mellow, satisfied smile. "But it's worked out very well, hasn't it? Elliot is a brilliant young man with a first-rate character. He's a dedicated public servant with great things ahead of him. As I said, I feel very proud of him."

"In that time when you had your doubts, did you investigate Elliot's background?"

His face tautened. "Why would I do a thing like that?"

"As a normal precaution. Elliot was something of a man of mystery, wasn't he?"

"There was no mystery about Elliot," Wren said emphatically. "He was, very clearly, a fine young man."

"Didn't you check out his school record? His service record?"

He leaned forward on the desk and glared at me. "What are they saying about him?" he whispered intensely. "What have you heard?"

"I haven't heard anything, Senator," I replied mildly.

I realized I had gone too far. The mannequin had come to life. The wide blue eyes were bright with anger.

"Let me tell you something, young man." His voice had a bitter edge to it. "When you're in public life, when you're trying to serve, there are always people who'll fling dirt at you. Envious, petty, malicious people!"

I heard the door of the office open. I turned in my chair and looked behind me. A black man in a chauffeur's uniform stood in the doorway. He was middle-aged, with a pencil-thin, gray mustache. His eyes flickered almost imperceptibly as he quickly took me in.

"I'll be with you in a minute, Ernest," Wren said. His voice was calm again. "Ernest has come to drive me home," he explained. The chauffeur turned to go. "Oh, Ernest," Wren said, "would you mail these for me, please?" He picked up the sealed envelopes.

"Yes, sir." Ernest took the envelopes from Wren and went out.

"I think our conversation is finished," Wren said.

"Thank you for talking with me, Senator," I said, rising.

I bent over to grind out my cigarette in the ashtray on the desk. As I did so, I took a quick look at the letter at Wren's elbow, the one he was answering. The full date was at the upper-right-hand corner—"September 24, 1963."

I looked at Wren again. He was staring at me. His facial muscles had sagged and suddenly he seemed twenty years older, a very old man. There was no life in his features, except for an indistinct spark that was quickening in his eyes.

"You won't find anything," he said. "Tell Thurston that. There's nothing to find."

I recognized the look in his eyes now. It was deep fear.

four

1   "Do you believe in destiny?" Elliot Karp asked.

"No," I said, "I don't."

"Neither do I. Destiny is just your conception of yourself. Maybe no one else sees it. Maybe it doesn't even make sense. But if you see it clearly enough, if you believe in it strongly enough, you can make it happen. That's all," he concluded, with a shrug. "You make it happen."

"I take it you do believe in luck?"

He laughed. "Luck, yeah. Mustn't forget luck." He paused pensively. Karp in meditation seemed no more introspective than Karp conversing. His handsome, sun-tanned face didn't alter; no thought process rippled the bland surface. I had the feeling that, speaking or thinking, he rarely strayed from the safer shallows of his mind. "But then you make your luck, too, don't you?"

He shifted his position, winced slightly, then adjusted the little pillow that supported the small of his back. He obviously would have been more comfortable in the swivel chair behind his desk, but he had insisted that we sit side by side on the leather couch.

From a framed photograph on top of a bookcase, Penelope and her baby boy smiled down at us. The child, who seemed about a year old in this picture, was faced forward on his mother's lap. He was very blond, adorable, and he was laughing gleefully at the camera.

"Ever since I was a little kid," Karp went on, "I've had this image. I've seen myself in a big office like this, with good people around me—" his gesture indicated the men and women in the smaller offices on the periphery—" all of us involved in something important." He put his hand on my knee and leaned closer. "And what this administration is doing *is* important, Don," he intoned earnestly. "Not only to New York, but to every major city in the country. New York, as always, is ahead of everyone—in the bad as well as the good. The urban problems hit here first. That means we have to find the solutions first."

I nodded sagely, wondering at the same time why it sounded so familiar? Then I remembered. I had read it in a clipping. Karp had just recited, word for word, one of his earliest statements to the press.

"When you were a kid," I asked, "and you had this image, did you have any idea that you'd eventually end up in city planning?"

"Hell, no! I didn't know nothin'," he said, his smile good-natured, his double negative droll. "I was just like any other dumb kid. All I did was go out for sports and have a good time. I figured that, whatever my life's work was going to be, I'd probably back into it, anyway. And that's pretty much the way it's worked out." For all his phoniness, Karp seemed to have a quite genuine modesty. Or, at least, he had no illusions about his natural gifts. It was his most engaging trait. "And yet, like I said," he went on, "I just *knew* I'd end up doing something important. I don't know why. I guess my mother put it into my head. She's of that immigrant generation that bought the American Dream a hundred per cent. When she told me I could grow up to be President someday, she thought she was telling me God's honest truth." He laughed. "She didn't know much about the political realities."

"Maybe Vice-President," I said.

He looked at me with sudden interest, as if the idea had never occurred to him. "You think so? You think the country's ready for it?"

"Within another decade or so. Of course," I added, "I don't know what your timetable is."

"Hey, Don, you're putting ideas into my head!" He slapped my knee genially. "You're as bad as my mom."

In this chummy moment, I looked right into his eyes. They were as empty as ever. The lines around his eyes were deep, but not with amusement; rather, with that subtle tension I had noticed when I first met him.

Karp looked away quickly. "Anyway," he said, "I had this sense of something big in my future. So I kind of stayed loose, kept myself open for it. That's why I didn't really stick with anything I did. For instance, when I was living in L.A., I had a good job as sales manager for Telextron, a nice solid company that makes business machines. Now, there's nothing wrong with selling business machines. But it just didn't seem important enough. It didn't fit in with my conception of myself. And, one day, there I was, with six phones on my desk, talking on one, two of them on hold, and another one ringing, and suddenly I thought, This is for the birds! So I wrote out my letter of resignation and moved on."

"And then you met Penelope," I said.

"Yeah. Talk about luck!" Quickly, he qualified. "I mean, even if I'd never met Penelope and her father, I would have made it—one way or the other. But Penelope was a whole lot more than I'd ever expected. She's the most fabulous woman in the world." His voice became hushed with wonder. "Sometimes I lie awake at night, and I think of Penelope lying there asleep in the next room—and I say to myself, Ellie, you've gotten lucky! You've gotten real lucky!"

"You sleep in separate bedrooms?"

He looked at me sharply. "As a matter of fact, we do. You want to know if I sleep in the nude, too?"

"Do you?"

"I wear pajamas." His smile was tight now. "And I sleep alone because of my back. I have a special orthopedic bed."

There was a knock on the door. "Come in," Karp called out. A gray-haired, expressionless man in shirt sleeves entered.

"What can I do for you, Sam?" Karp asked, rising. With a wave of his hand, he introduced us. "Mr. Skelton, Mr. Herndon. Sam is my chief engineer."

Herndon barely looked at me. He gave me a perfunctory nod, then fixed his gaze once again on Karp. "Have you read Berg's report yet?" he asked.

"I haven't gotten around to it. I will."

"We can't delay that requisition much longer, Elliot."

There was a stolidness to Herndon as he stood there. And Karp's smile was a little too pleasant. They seemed a mismatched pair; the fat, middle-aged civil servant in his wilted, white Arrow shirt, and the tall, lean, young politician in his expensive gray tweed jacket and custom-made pink shirt. I imagined I was witnessing some minor showdown between them. It was muted, not particularly tense; perhaps it was something that happened all the time.

Karp went to his desk. He searched through a stack of papers and drew out a document, some eight or ten pages in thickness—Berg's report, I assumed. Without removing the paper clip, he flipped through it. He didn't seem to be skimming it so much as evaluating the typing. "Do these figures add up?" he asked.

"They add up," Herndon said.

Karp took another paper from the pile, a single-sheet form with the spaces filled in, and swiftly signed it. He held it out to Herndon. "Here's your requisition," he said.

Herndon took the paper. His lips curled, ever so slightly, but tactlessly; it was as if it were no longer worth the effort to him to conceal his contempt. "Thanks, Elliot," he said. He departed.

"You've got to keep on your toes with these guys," Karp said. "Bureaucrats, you know? Paper pushers! If you don't watch it, they'll bury you up to your neck in memos and reports. You can get more accomplished with one face-to-face talk than with ten thousand words of *this* bullshit." He dismissed the pile of papers with a scornful flick of his fingertips. "Now, if you don't mind, Don, I'm going to have to cut this short. I've got some dictation to do." He sat behind the desk, picked up the telephone receiver, and buzzed his secretary.

"May I ask one last question?"

"Go ahead." His fingers drummed on the desk lightly as he waited for his secretary to respond.

"You're not a man of independent means, are you?"

"No, I'm not."

"And a public official's salary isn't all that much?"

"It certainly isn't."

"Then don't you ever regret sacrificing your chances to make big money?"

"Not at all. I haven't sacrificed a thing." He buzzed his secretary again, impatiently this time.

"Money means nothing to you?"

"I didn't say that. As a matter of fact, money means a lot to me. But any guy with a brain in his head should be able to make a pile, if he wants to."

"Oh? What's the secret?"

"There's no secret." Karp leaned forward and thrust his finger at me, the classic forceful-executive pose. "The market, Don! It's one hell of an exciting ball game! If a man's smart—I mean, *really* smart—he can make ten million in two years."

"You've been playing the market—and you're ahead?"

"In the end, I'll be ahead. Way ahead." He looked at the receiver in his hand and his face darkened with annoyance. He hung up abruptly. "Look, on your way out, if you see my girl, could you tell her to come in here?"

As I left the office, I did, in fact, see Karp's secretary. She was busily emptying the drawers of her desk.

"Mr. Karp wants you," I told her, "for some dictation."

"Tell the pasha to learn how to type," she said.

I was somewhat taken aback. "What kind of attitude is that?"

"It is the attitude of someone who is leaving this place forever." She picked up a little china puppy dog, the one ornament on her desk, and dropped it into her tote bag. "This is my last day."

"The job didn't work out?"

"The job was fine." She emphasized the word "job," distinguishing it from the unspoken word "people." "I did my work."

"I don't doubt it," I said. "I'm sure you're a very good secretary."

"I am a sensational secretary—which Mr. Karp knows. I am also a human being—which he sometimes forgets."

"And so you've quit?"

"I've quit."

She slammed the emptied drawers of the desk shut, quite violently. She had barely looked at me; in fact, she seemed hardly aware of me other than as some convenient ear that had happened by. But still I lingered. I had long ago

learned never to pass up a disgruntled employee. And I was
intrigued by her reference to Karp as "the pasha," with its
suggestion of sexual hanky-panky.

"What's your name?" I asked.

She straightened up and looked at me. The warm interest
in my voice startled her into a smile. "Gwen," she replied,
brushing back a stray strand of hair. "Gwen Cooper."

She was young and bosomy, particularly so in the skin-
tight sweater she was wearing. Her hair was bleached a little
too blonde for her dark coloring, her eyes were overdone with
green eye shadow, but, all in all, she was a well-put-together
working girl; one who was still searching, as was clearly evi-
dent in the intentness of her gaze on me. "And you're Don
Skelton?"

"That's right."

"Why does your name sound familiar to me?"

"You may have seen my by-line. I write for newspapers
and magazines."

"What do you write about?"

"Movie stars," I answered casually.

"Honestly? Like who?"

"Steve McQueen—Robert Redford—" I said, shamelessly
wrapping myself in borrowed charisma.

I had her going now. Her eyes were bright with the fan's
delirium. "What's Robert Redford really like?"

"Why don't I tell you over a drink after work?"

"All right," she said, with a pleased little down-and-up
lilt in her voice.

"What time are you finishing here?"

"About five."

"Meet you in the lobby at five."

"All right," she said again.

On my way to the elevators, I encountered Herndon,
the chief engineer. He was coming out of the men's room.

"Hi," he muttered, when he found himself face to face with me. He started to walk on.

"I had a pleasant talk with your boss," I said quickly, brightly, forcing him to stop.

Herndon turned and looked at me. "Elliot is a pleasant man," he said carefully.

"I sure was impressed with him as an administrator," I went on. "That requisition—I don't know what it was, but he took care of it just like *that*, didn't he? Does he always get things done that fast?"

An incredulous look came into Herndon's eyes. Evidently, he took my show of naïveté at face value. "Sometimes," he replied. "And sometimes not." After a moment, he asked, "Are you doing a story on Elliot?"

"No, I'm writing a piece on his wife. But there's always a chance I might do something on Mr. Karp, too. That is," I added, "if he turns out to be interesting enough."

I could see the uncertainty in his expression as he tried to interpret this last casually tossed-off line. Was he imagining it or was there a hidden implication in my words? "There's a lot that's interesting about Elliot," he ventured.

"I'm sure there is," I said.

He was teetering on the edge now. I recognized that look —the slightly wild-eyed look of a potential informant who is about to give in to temptation. A little more encouragement, perhaps, and he would say that little thing, whatever it was, those few deadly words that might undercut a despised superior, might alter a condition of hateful subservience.

"Have you worked at this agency long?" I asked.

"Twenty-two years," he said.

"Is Mr. Karp very different from the other directors you've worked under?"

"Political appointees are all pretty much the same," Herndon said. He paused. "But, yes, Elliot is—special."

"Oh?" I waited.

"Ask him about the variance on the Broadway block front," he said suddenly. "Ask him about it sometime."

"I don't know what you mean."

"He should have approved that variance six months ago. Ask him why he won't let it go through." He looked away uneasily. "But don't say I was the one who mentioned it."

Herndon ducked his head and hurried off.

2 Gwen Cooper wasn't very hard to dazzle. I treated her to inside glimpses of the superstars, short takes of how they seemed and what they did when I interviewed them—Jane Fonda smoking pot in her living room, Steve McQueen wandering off to his back yard and firing a rifle into the air.

Gwen listened raptly, openmouthed. She bought the magic of it totally. We were sitting in a coffeehouse-tavern in SoHo, a cavernous place with exposed brick walls, surrounded by bearded young men and girls in jeans and jerseys, with a Carly Simon record on the jukebox, and trucks snorting grumpily outside; yet it was as if the brightness in her eyes were the reflection of the flames of a campfire and I were some Homeric bard chanting tales of the gods—anthropomorphic gods, who fornicated and bickered just like ordinary mortals, but supernatural beings, nonetheless.

All except for one. "Penelope Wren," she repeated scornfully, when I brought up her name. "What's so special about *her?*"

"Have you ever met her?"

"No, I haven't. But Elliot talks a lot about her."

"Well, she's a very beautiful woman."

"She looks all right, I suppose—judging from her pictures." Gwen, clearly, wasn't too impressed. "But she's just some snooty society lady, that's all. She doesn't have it. No, sir," she said firmly, "she just doesn't have it."

"What makes you think that?"

She smiled meaningfully. "If a woman has it, her man doesn't go looking elsewhere."

"Elliot has an eye for the ladies?"

"He gets around," she said vaguely.

"He's had affairs, huh?"

She ran her finger around the rim of her glass non-chalantly. "Maybe. And maybe not."

I couldn't tell whether she was being coy or discreet. Either way, she could keep me fishing for hours.

"So, okay," I said, "he flirts. We all do. That doesn't mean he really *does* anything. If *I* had a gorgeous woman like Penelope Wren for my wife, why would I bother? I mean, how could I improve on her?"

As I had hoped, I got a rise out of her. Her overdone eyes narrowed to sludgy fringes. "You think this Penelope is pretty great, don't you?"

"I'm one of her greatest admirers. To me, she's some kind of—goddess."

"What would you say if I told you that this goddess of yours was frigid?" she said, her voice cutting. "That she's never had an orgasm? Probably never will?"

"That's more than you can possibly know from office chitchat with your boss."

"We've talked other places than the office."

I was briefly silent; I felt embarrassed, actually. I was shocked, as I always was, that a woman should so lightly bandy about another woman's most private sexual problems. There were some confidences that even I respected.

Gwen seemed pleased by the impact of her little revelation. She sat back and took a swallow of her drink; an Alexander, a chocolate slop of liqueur. When she lowered the glass, a brown halo was left above her upper lip. "You ever been married?" she asked.

We were back to basics now; the mating gleam was in

Gwen's eyes. I was careful to return her look with a small, shy smile. "No, not yet."

"How have you managed to escape this long? A smart, good-looking guy like you?"

"There was a girl once—" I let my voice trail off. A hint of a tragic romance in one's past is sure-fire with certain unsophisticated mentalities.

"Dead?" Gwen asked, her eyes moist with compassion.

"Oh, no," I replied quickly. Obviously, I had overdone the pathos a bit. "She found someone else."

She reached out and squeezed my hand reassuringly. "Maybe it was for the best," she said. She sat back again and appraised me for a moment. "So you're a writer," she said. "My girl friend Shirley dates a writer."

"Anyone I know?"

"Maybe. He works for the *Variety Store Merchandiser.*"

"No, then I probably don't know him."

"Who do *you* work for?"

"No one. I'm free-lance."

She looked a bit perplexed. "Then what do you do for a living?"

"Well, you know, they *pay* me for the things I write."

She glanced at my clothes—the expensive English woolen of my jacket, the Cardin tie—and smiled faintly, thoughtfully. I could tell she was getting a new reading on me. Rich dilettante. Inherited money. I was looking better to her all the time.

"I'm glad I've gotten to know you, Gwen," I said at length, gazing into her eyes. "I mean, I'm *really* glad now. When I asked you out, I was just trying to cheer you up. But—"

"Cheer me up?" she broke in. "Why?"

"Because you seemed so upset about leaving your job."

"I was *not* upset," she said emphatically. "I couldn't have been happier."

"Oh, you're putting on a brave face, Gwen, I know. But I can tell how bitter you are. For instance, the way you talk against Elliot's wife—even though you don't know her—and you don't know *him* that well, either."

"I know Elliot *very* well," she said, indignant at this challenge to her credentials.

"But you were just his secretary, weren't you?"

"I wasn't *just* his secretary. I was a lot more than that to Elliot."

I gave her an incredulous look. "You don't mean to say—you had a thing with him?"

She looked at me uncertainly. "Would it shock you if I said yes?"

"Oh, no," I reassured her, "I'd understand. We're both sophisticated people, after all."

"Elliot and I," she began, "had a—" She hesitated. "Well, I don't want to say affair. Affair sounds kind of sordid, you know? We had a romance," she said, more positively. "A beautiful romance. And I have no regrets. If I regret anything, it's that—" She broke off.

"That what?"

"—that Elliot lacks the maturity to have a truly meaning-ful relationship."

"Was he the one who ended the romance?"

"*I* did," Gwen said, more sharply. "I couldn't go on with it. The situation became—" she shrugged—"impossible." She brooded for a moment. Then, with sudden fierceness, she burst out, "I don't take *anyone's* leftovers. No, sir! Other girls might. Not me."

"You mean you got upset because of his wife."

"I'm not talking about his wife," she said, and lapsed into silence, as if she wanted to pursue the subject no further.

To keep the thing going, I threw out the first question that came to my mind. "Where would the two of you meet? Your place?"

"No," she replied. "We couldn't do that. I've got a room-mate. We'd meet at his apartment. His bachelor apartment—he still has it. He even gave me a key." With a sour smile, she added, "That was his mistake. If I hadn't had that key, I *still* wouldn't know any better."

"So what do you know now?"

"I know that Elliot Karp is a disturbed person," she said gravely, "with a deep-seated insecurity and a childish need to prove his virility."

"And how did you find that out?" I asked.

"I forgot my umbrella."

"Pardon?"

"I left it at Elliot's place one night. A couple of days later, when I got up to go to work, it was raining. I needed the umbrella, so I went over to get it. I didn't expect he'd be there, but I had the key." She grimaced wryly. "He was there, all right—with company. The two of them were having break-fast. They weren't even dressed yet."

"Must have been embarrassing for Elliot."

"Oh, he's so smooth, that guy. He didn't turn a hair. He pretended I'd come to get a paper he had in his briefcase. And I went along with it. God, I felt like an idiot!"

"What did the woman say?"

"She didn't say anything. I guess she felt pretty stupid, too."

"You find out who she was?"

"Not then, later. She called the office a couple of times. I recognized her voice—she had a foreign accent of some kind. Her name is Margaret."

"Margaret who?"

Gwen looked at me askance. "Why do you want to know? You writing a book?"

"Just for the sake of gossip, that's all," I said, smiling disingenuously. "Never mind. It's not important."

"I don't remember, anyway. Wait a minute," she said,

her face suddenly intent, "it's on the tip of my tongue." She concentrated, but it eluded her. "No," she said, finally, shaking her head.

"And this is why you quit your job?" I asked. "Because you found out that Elliot was two-timing you?"

"It wasn't just that. It's a good job, I hate to give it up. But I can't take the—the *humiliation*. I mean, after it was over, he acted like I'd never meant anything to him. He treated me like I was just another piece of furniture around the office." The corners of her mouth turned down unhappily. "Elliot's got a short memory, I guess."

"It's also not very smart of him to treat you that way. You've been his secretary for a while, haven't you?"

"Since he was appointed, yeah."

"You must know a few things about Elliot," I said, "things his enemies would like to know."

Gwen's mouth tightened. "If I did, I wouldn't tell anyone. I'm not a fink."

Her statement was just a touch too emphatic. It was probably the first time it had occurred to her that she had weapons she could use against her callous ex-lover.

"You're being more decent about this whole thing than Elliot is," I commented.

"That's not hard to do," she said.

I leaned forward and put my hand over hers. "You're a good person, Gwen." She squeezed my hand in response. "I'd like to see you again. I've some work to do tonight. But why don't we get together tomorrow evening?"

"All right," she said, with the down-and-up lilt in her voice.

"We'll have dinner. And maybe we'll take in some entertainment afterward. Who shall it be? Bobby Short? Mabel Mercer?"

"Either one," she said brightly.

"It's a date." I signaled for the check.

Gwen redid her mouth while I checked the waitress's addition and figured out the tip. "Oh!" she said suddenly, lowering her compact mirror and lipstick. "I remember."

"Remember what?"

"That woman's name. It was Hivnor. Margaret Hivnor."

I stared at her, astonished. "You mean *Margrit* Hivnor?"

Gwen looked a bit perplexed. "That's what I said. Margaret Hivnor. You know her?"

"I thought I did," I said, casual again. "But I was thinking of someone else." I put down some bills and rose. "Let's go."

3 At home, among my mail, there was a letter from Telextron, Inc. in Los Angeles. I opened it immediately.

Dear Mr. Skelton:

Re your letter of the 15th, I have checked our records and your information seems to be incorrect. No person named Elliot Karp has ever been employed as the sales manager for Telextron. An Elliot Karp was a member of our sales force from March to October of 1966. I see that his work record was good and that he resigned of his own volition. Beyond that, I can tell you nothing further at this time.

I hope this is a satisfactory answer to your inquiry.

Sincerely,

David Crawford
Personnel Director

The letter came as no great surprise. I mixed a Scotch-and-soda and settled into the armchair with the Elliot Karp file. I flipped through it aimlessly, ignoring the text of the clippings, simply taking in the photographs. There were quite a few of them; Karp was probably the most photographed official in the Mayor's administration. I was struck by the fact that, no matter what the occasion and mood, whether he was addressing a news conference or standing at bat in a Central Park softball game, Karp's expression was exactly the same— the nice-guy, mild smile, the candid, open-eyed gaze—and the whole of the expression looking superimposed, as if it had been freshly stamped on a pristine blank of flesh.

I remembered what Blake Hivnor had said—*If you dig into Elliot Karp deep enough, you'll discover he isn't there. He's just a figment of his own imagination.* That had proved to be true enough. The economics graduate–naval officer–business executive had disintegrated at the first probing. It had been a hopelessly flimsy artifact, actually; nothing that could have been expected to stand up to serious testing. Elliot Karp, in fact, was no mystery at all. He was a phony; the tinny ring could be detected in everything he said and did. At the most, he was a fluke, a case of a loser's fantasy freakishly fulfilled.

And yet there *were* mysteries, mysteries that had nothing to do with Karp as a person, and they were starting to bother me. There was Blake, for instance. When I had learned that Harry Thurston was the new owner of *View*, I had thought that at last I comprehended the real purpose of the assignment. This hatchet job was to be Blake's love offering to his fascistic employer; he would deliver the severed head of the Mayor's lieutenant. It was rough stuff, but it was the way the game was played, and I could accept it.

But now, within the last hour, I had discovered that Blake's wife, Margrit, had been Karp's mistress; and suddenly everything was in doubt again. Gwen Cooper presumably had been referring to the recent past, to an event that postdated the Hivnors' separation. But Karp's affair with Margrit Hivnor could have been going on for a long time. Did Blake know of it? Was it responsible for the breakup of his marriage?

Perhaps this assignment had nothing to do with Harry

Thurston. Perhaps it had nothing to do with any power game at all. Perhaps I was simply serving as the instrument for a spiteful act of private revenge.

Well, in the long run, it didn't matter. Whatever Blake's personal reasons, the article was a legitimate one; the further I went, the more valid it seemed. A fraud was holding a high office, the kind of high office that, with its golden opportunities for graft, had corrupted many honest men before him. It was inconceivable that someone as congenitally dishonest as Karp would have passed up these opportunities. All I had to do was turn over a few stones and I would find it, the hunk of dirt I needed, Karp's rank little rip-off, whatever it was. Then I would have my piece, a piece that would alert the public and scare the bejesus out of an overly complacent set of politicians.

Yet the larger mystery remained. There were easy answers I could find and would find. But I would still be no closer to an answer to the most perplexing question of all. It was, quite simply, How did Elliot Karp get away with it?

I found myself looking at a particular news photograph in the file. I took it out to examine it more closely. It was a picture of the chirstening of Elliot Karp, Jr. The Mayor, who was the godfather, was holding the swaddled infant in his arms. The smiling parents, Penelope and Karp, stood on either side. At the edge of the picture, the Episcopalian minister had his hand upraised, as if in benediction.

All but one were in perfect key with the moment: the Mayor was looking down at the infant, as reverential as a Magi; Penelope was as incandescent as any joyful new mother; the minister was as solemn as if he truly believed he was God's proxy.

It was Karp who stood out from the others, stood out as the one false note in the composition. Even on this sacramental occasion, this ritual passing on of his name to his own son, his face still had that same superimposed expression it had in all his other photographs, that manufactured smile and vaguely uncomfortable look, as if he knew he didn't really belong there, as if he were merely some stranger who had been pulled in off the street to witness the ceremony.

Why couldn't they see it? I wondered. It was so plain what he was! Yet these good people—this well-meaning mayor, this beautiful princess—accepted him totally, unquestioningly. It seemed the most perverse kind of blindness. Could it be there was some flaw of innocence in the American upper class? Some childlike trust in appearance?

I was a lower-middle-class type from the West and I had been raised to have faith in the justice of things. *In the long run, you get what you deserve,* my father would say, and he really believed it, in his despairing way.

In his own eyes, he was a failure. Through most of his adult years, until the shake in his hands got too bad, my father was a draftsman at Lockheed, a good worker, steadily employed. But he had built no dams, he had thrown no bridges over waterways, he had never come close to being the Great Engineer of his childhood dreams. And, manfully, he blamed himself for it. He didn't blame the Depression, which had forced him to quit college; he didn't blame the early marriage, which had narrowed his already limited options. The fault, as he was always quick to admit, lay not in his stars, but in himself. *You're either born with it, Don, or you're not. It's like some people, no matter how hard they try, can only jump five feet high. Other people can jump seven. You've got to have the muscles for it, that's all. Those men at the top, they've got the right muscles. They can't fake it.* And, having settled this question to his satisfaction, he drank himself to death at fifty-six.

I had accepted my father's premise readily enough. I had my particular muscles, too, my strengths—a facility with words, a nose for the truth, a high tolerance for solitude. And I had fashioned a career of sorts, a rather thin one, but, whatever I had, I had earned.

Yet here was this guy, this Elliot Karp, an untalented drifter who had come from out of nowhere and lied and lied and won it all. It shouldn't be that easy. It mustn't be that easy. It would make a joke out of a million desperate, obscure lives, my father's life, my own, if there was nothing more to it than that.

The phone rang. I put down the file, rose, and crossed to answer it.

I almost didn't recognize the voice. It was Sally, but her tone was strangely constricted; each word was forced out very evenly, as if a great weight of control was bearing down on every syllable. "Thanks a lot, darling," she said. "I knew I could depend on you."

"What are you talking about?"

"I've just been fired."

"What?" For a moment, I was too stunned to say anything. "But why? You're great at your job."

"Yeah. But I made a mistake."

"What mistake?"

"I made the mistake of leaving you alone with a certain client at a certain lunch at Sardi's."

"How did your boss find out about that?"

"How do you think? Penelope told him."

"That's a lousy thing for her to do," I said, after a moment.

"Isn't it? Well, *you're* her fan. I'm not."

"So, just because of that, your boss gave you notice?"

"Nothing that fancy. He told me to gather up my things and get out."

"But that's not fair! You're not to blame if—"

"Yes," she cut in, *"we* know that, don't we, Don?"

"Look, Sally, this isn't the end of the world. I'll come right over and we'll—"

"I'm not going to see you any more."

"Come on, honey, let me try to help you! I'll call around. I guarantee you, in a few days I'll get you a *better* job."

"Don't do me any favors, lover." She hung up.

It felt no more real than any other good-by in my life. And no less. I felt no sense of loss, no hurt. I simply felt slightly sick.

Had I known she was going to be fired? The truth of it was, I hadn't thought about it. Not once.

Even now, I didn't dwell on it. Instead, I thought of slighter things. For instance, Sally's birthday. It was coming up next week. She would have laid a thousand to one I wouldn't remember. I was going to surprise her.

Well, she was the one who had surprised me.

I was alone again. That was the plain fact of it. I was alone again and it wasn't going to be easy. After each bungled romance, it got harder.

I went back to the armchair. The photograph of the christening lay on the side table. From his place at the right of the group, Elliot Karp smiled up at me, the valued public servant, friend of the Mayor, husband of Penelope, father of Elliot junior.

You're a thief, you smug son of a bitch, I thought. I'm going to make you eat shit.

five

1 Shortly before noon, the doorbell rang. I hadn't been expecting anyone, but I buzzed the house door open, anyway. I could have gone down the one flight of stairs to check out my unknown caller, but I wasn't usually that cautious or that fearful, never having been mugged or otherwise assaulted in my years in the city.

I opened my door and called out, "Who is it?" I heard light footsteps coming up the stairs, so light they could have been those of a child playing a stalking game.

I went to the head of the stairs and looked down. On the fifth stair from the top, Penelope Wren stopped abruptly, as if I were the one who had surprised her. "Hello," she said.

"Hello."

"I came down to the Village to do some shopping," she said, "and I happened to be walking along this street—" Her light, casual gesture pointed up the airiness of the whim that had led her to my door.

"Well, this is a pleasant surprise," I said. "Come in."

I showed her into my apartment. In the living room, she turned to me and smiled apologetically. "Am I interrupting you in your work?"

"Not at all. I was being lazy. Would you like some coffee?"

"No, thanks. I won't be staying that long." Penelope took off her coat and gave it to me. I now saw that she was wearing a rich-hippie outfit, a blouse and slacks combination that was styled in imitation of a cowboy's faded blue denims, the sort of thing an uptown socialite would wear to go shopping in the Village—or to drop in on a Village writer. She went to my most uncomfortable straight-backed chair and sat.

I sat opposite her. We regarded each other silently for a few moments. "Do you know the Carltons?" Penelope asked, at length.

"No. Should I?"

"They live on this block. The pink brownstone near the corner."

"The only person I know on this block is the Chinese laundryman. *He's* my sense of community. New York," I added wryly, the two words that always explained everything.

"New York," she repeated, echoing my tone. She watched as I lit a cigarette. "May I have a cigarette, too, please?"

"Sure." I went to her and flipped a cigarette up from the pack. She took it. "I didn't know you smoked," I said.

"I don't—usually. This will be it for today." I lit her cigarette. Her eyes didn't rise to meet mine for the usual moment of man-woman eye contact; instead, she seemed to be studying my gold Dunhill. "Nice lighter," she commented.

"A friend of mine gave it to me." I paused. "Sally Fry."

She glanced up at me now, very briefly.

I sat again. Penelope took a shallow puff of her cigarette, stopping just short of an inhale. She looked past me, at the open doorway that led to my study. "You work in there?" she asked.

"Yes."

"How's it going?" Her tone had changed subtly.

"The article? It's shaping up."

"Finding out what you want to know?"

"There's nothing to find out, as such," I said carefully. "Just what you tell me. And what other people tell me."

"About me?" The "me" was stressed slightly, just enough to convey a polite skepticism.

"About you, of course."

Penelope looked at me silently for a moment. Her gaze was more direct than it had ever been before, and colder. "You know, Don, sometimes I get the funny feeling that you and Blake are trying to pull a dirty trick on us."

I kept my face expressionless. "Why should you think that?"

"It's just a feeling," she said. I caught the note of uncertainty in her voice and I realized that, in fact, she still didn't know. She was going on very slight evidence, perhaps nothing more than intuition. "You went to see my father?"

"That's right."

"Daddy told me that you seemed a lot more interested in Elliot than you did in me."

"We happened to start talking about Elliot, that's all," I said, with a shrug.

Her gaze held on me, unwavering. "Your friend—Sally—told me to be extremely careful with you. She thought you were up to something."

"That was very self-sacrificing of her," I said.

"Self-sacrificing? It was her job."

"Yes, it *was* her job. She no longer has it—thanks to you."

"She's been let go?" Penelope seemed genuinely surprised. "You didn't insist that she be fired?"

"I fired the firm, not her."

"Same thing."

"Miss Fry was derelict in her duty," Penelope said coolly. "It couldn't be overlooked." She might have been speaking of some inadequate maid who had neglected too many dusty surfaces. "Anyway," she went on, "I didn't think it was a good idea to have as my press agent a young woman who also happened to be your—" She smiled faintly. "Is there a nice word for it?"

"Is there something *not* nice about 'girl friend'?"

" 'Mistress' is the more grown-up term, isn't it?" she purred.

I sensed that she was enjoying this part of our conversation. I began to get angry. This haughty princess could throw a working girl onto the unemployment line without a qualm. It didn't concern her, since Sally wasn't quite a person in her eyes, any more than I was. And yet, at the same time, she took a more than proper interest, a feline interest, in our sex lives. It was as if it charmed her that the dirty beggars did, indeed, fornicate.

Suddenly I was sick of the entire deception, the meek imposture that had been forced on me. And, sharply, I asked, "Why do you feel you have to protect this husband of yours?"

Her face went blank. "Because he *is* my husband," she answered simply.

"And he's a great man?"

"Yes, he is."

"You don't even know him," I said disgustedly.

Penelope said nothing. Her eyes were wary and she simply waited for me to reveal myself further.

I had gone too far, I realized. In one petulant moment, I had just about blown the whole thing.

"Look, Penelope," I said, "believe me, I'm writing this piece about you. *You* are my subject. But I'm a journalist and I have the instincts of a journalist. And if, along the way, I come upon interesting, unexpected information, then I just have to follow it up. It doesn't mean I use any of it. I just file it away for future reference."

"Future reference?" she echoed questioningly.

The implied threat in my last words had been quite accidental. But I let it stand. I still needed her co-operation, and subtle extortion was possibly the only means I had left to make sure of it.

"But I don't understand," Penelope said, with a perplexed frown. "What could you have found out about myself—or Elliot—that's so interesting and unexpected?"

"You really want me to tell you?"

"Yes, please, tell me."

Her voice was gentle, but the challenge was unmistakable. And I had to meet it. If I backed down, I knew I would lose all my leverage in the situation.

"Elliot is something of an imposter," I said. "He's faked his entire background."

There was a slight tensing of the muscles around her eyes. And that was all. "Go on," she said.

"For one thing, Elliot never graduated from college. He dropped out—or flunked out. And he wasn't a naval officer. He was never in the service at all. Also, he was not the sales manager of Telextron, Inc. He was never anything more glorious than a traveling salesman."

Penelope gazed at me thoughtfully, with unruffled calm. "Your information isn't completely correct," she said.

"You think I'm making this all up?"

"No. But it isn't *completely* correct," she said, more precisely. "Elliot didn't flunk out of college. Nor did he intentionally drop out. He planned to be out of school for only a year or so. But financial difficulties—he had to look after his mother, you know—kept him from completing his education."

I felt deflated and a little foolish. "I see you know all about it. Of course. You *are* married to the man, after all."

"I knew it *before* I married him."

"What? You mean, he's concocted this story since then?"

"No, that's not true, either." Choosing her words carefully, she explained. "Elliot has always been a little—fanciful about his early years. You can hardly blame him—he had such bad luck. But, when we got married, Elliot had no secrets from me."

"He told you the whole truth from the beginning?"

"Yes." I detected the awkwardness in the way she answered, a touch of overemphasis. It was just enough to give away that it was a lie.

"I don't believe it," I said. "I don't believe that Elliot simply told you."

Penelope looked suddenly uncomfortable. She was capable of living a large illusion. But it embarrassed her to be caught in a small untruth. "No, not exactly," she admitted. "You see, Daddy hired private detectives to investigate Elliot. That's how it all came out."

"Then I don't understand," I said. "You discovered all this about him and yet you still went ahead and married him?"

She rose quickly, crossed to the sofa, and picked up her coat. "I told you I wouldn't stay long," she said, smiling brightly.

I got up and went to her, meaning to help her with the coat. She managed to slip into it before my hands touched her. She hurried to the door.

"I hope you're not angry," I said.

She turned back. "Angry? Of course not. I'm just a little surprised. I'm surprised to learn that you're such a snob. I would think that you, Don, of all people, wouldn't judge a man by his antecedents."

It could only have been a wild thrust; she knew nothing about me. Yet I felt the blood rise to my cheeks.

Penelope opened the door. Then, as if it were an after-thought, she said, "As for your question, I married Elliot because I loved him. And he has never given me cause to regret it. I'm very proud of him."

She went out. It was a clean exit. The door tapped shut after her as crisp as a handclap.

And I realized that, like a clumsy supporting player, I had been outclassed. I had learned little more than I already knew about her and Elliot Karp. But Penelope had learned exactly what she needed to know about me.

2 "I have something to confess," I said.

Gwen made an indistinct sound in her throat and curled up to me more snugly. I couldn't see her face, only a mass of teased curls in the region of my armpit, then a stretch of bare back, and the arc of her buttock.

"I'm not what I seem," I said.

Her face emerged from some recess of my upper body. "You're married?"

"No, I'm not married."

She propped herself on one elbow and squinted at me. "You like guys?"

"Jesus, I've just balled you twice and you ask me if I'm a fag?"

"I went with a guy who had that problem," Gwen said. "He'd just gotten over a heavy affair with a fella. And he was terrific in bed. Almost as good as you," she added diplomatically.

"Well, I don't happen to have that particular problem."

Gwen curled up beside me again. She had reaffirmed that I was single and heterosexual, and that was all that mattered to her. She put her hand lightly on my stomach, then started to slide it downward.

I gripped her wrist, gently but firmly, and set her hand aside. "Gwen," I said, "I'm an undercover agent."

She giggled. She evidently thought it was a *double-entendre.*

"No, seriously, Gwen."

She lifted her head. "You're an undercover agent?"

"That's right."

"What does that mean?"

"It means I'm carrying out an investigation. This business of my writing an article on Karp's wife—that's just a cover. I'm really working for the government."

"I thought you said you were a free-lance writer."

"I am. But that's not my *real* job. I'm a federal agent."

"Oh," she said softly, impressed. "Good." I think it gratified her to learn that I had steady employment, after all. "Then you're a narc or something like that?"

"I'm into something even more important." I sat up. "Gwen, we have to talk."

She sat up and regarded me solemnly. She crossed an arm over her bare breasts, as if it had suddenly struck her that it was unseemly to be so exposed before me.

"Gwen," I began gravely, "I know I don't have to ask you if you're a good citizen."

"Of course I'm a good citizen," she said, a bit defensively.

"And you feel a sense of responsibility to your community?"

"Yes," she insisted. "Yes, I do."

"Then listen," I said. "I can't tell you much about my investigation. But I can tell you this. There is corruption—big corruption—in this city's government!"

"I bet there is," she murmured fervently.

"It is corruption *so* big, *so* far-reaching, that it affects every man, woman, and child in this city. And some of us, myself, my buddies, are risking our necks day and night trying to do something about it."

I doubt that Redford or McQueen could have said the speech any more passionately. Gwen was the perfect audience for it. She was wide-eyed; her mouth had fallen open slightly.

"Now, I'm not saying that Elliott Karp is involved," I

went on. "We don't know. But there's a chance he is. He could be innocent—and, then again, he just might be the key figure. You worked for Karp a long time, Gwen, you were closer to him than anyone." More gently, I said, "I realize you may feel some sense of personal loyalty to him." She started to speak up, but before she could, I continued. "I understand and I sympathize. But this thing is more important than any personal feelings. There's too much at stake—for this city, for this country." I paused, then asked, "Are you ready to help us, Gwen?"

She swallowed and nodded.

"Then let me ask you this. Is there anything you know about Elliot Karp that might be useful to us? Has he been mixed up in anything illegal? Or has he had contact with any criminal types?"

Gwen thought for a long time. I could tell she wasn't faking it; she was really racking her brain. "No," she answered, finally. "Not that I know of."

"Has he done something out of the ordinary?" I persisted. "Something that might have struck you as a little odd?"

She concentrated again. "No," she said. "I can't think of anything."

That's just great, I thought. An expensive French dinner, drinks and cover charge at a nightclub, an hour of strenuous love-making—all for nothing!

"Just a minute," Gwen said suddenly. "There *was* something."

"Yeah?"

"Elliot used to get calls from this certain man," she said slowly. "A Mr. Richard White. And Elliot was—well, very secretive about them, you know? Like, he wouldn't accept a call from Mr. White if there was anyone in his office. And, when he did talk to him, he'd tell me to make sure no one came in."

"Was this unusual for Karp?"

"Not in itself, maybe. Important people called all the time
—the Mayor, the Police Commissioner, congressmen—and Elliot
usually took their calls in private. But this man, this Mr. White,
was different."

"Different in what way?"

"For one thing," she said, "I don't think he was using
his real name."

"What makes you think that?"

"Well, I cut in on their conversation once. Accidentally,
you know? And Elliot was calling this man 'Gabe,' not 'Richard.' " She was getting into the spirit of the thing and her voice
took on a hushed, conspiratorial tone. "So 'Richard White'
could have been an assumed name, huh?"

"Sounds like it," I said. "Did you listen to this conversation long?"

"Of course not. I wouldn't do a thing like that." She
seemed offended that I would impugn her secretarial discretion.

"From the little bit you heard, then, could you tell what
they were talking about?"

"No." She shrugged. "It meant nothing to me."

"You don't know who this Mr. White is? What he does?"

"I have no idea."

"And you never saw him, of course?"

"Yes, I did. Once."

"He came to the office?"

"No," she said, "it was at a restaurant." She paused to
get the details clear in her mind. "Elliot called me at lunch-
time and told me he needed some papers. He said they were
in a sealed envelope on his desk. He asked me to bring them
over to this particular restaurant—I don't remember the name,
I'd never heard of it. It was an Italian restaurant way over
on the West Side. So I went over there, and Elliot was having
lunch with three other men. One of the men—he was short,

fat, with gray hair—said something and I recognized his voice. You couldn't forget it. It was high and sharp. He sounded like an angry old woman. I said, 'Oh, you're Mr. White.' He waited a moment, then he said, 'That's right. I'm Richard White, How'd you guess?' I told him I knew his voice from hearing it on the phone. He said I had a good ear. And that was it. Elliot gave me his nice, sweet, get-lost smile—and I got out of there." Gwen looked at me uncertainly, somewhat uneasily, as if it had occurred to her that she might have been wasting my time with a totally pointless story. "Does any of this mean anything?" she asked.

"It might," I said. "It just possibly might." I gave her knee a grateful squeeze. "Thanks, Gwen. You're a brave girl."

She smiled proudly and sat up straight. It was a posture that happened to show off her large breasts to good advantage. Her nipples, I noticed, perhaps responding to my touch, had become erect.

"But you may have to be even braver in the future," I said. "Are you prepared for that?"

"What do you mean?"

"Let's say this secret meeting you witnessed turns out to be evidence of a crime. Would you testify in court?"

Everything about her sagged a little, the corners of her mouth, her shoulders, her nipples, and she was silent for a moment. But when, at length, she answered, her voice was firm. "Yes, I would."

3 The next morning, Jerry Gutman called. Without preamble, he said, "Let's get together and talk about Elliot Karp."

"Why?" I asked innocently. "You doing a story on him?"

"One of us is," Jerry said.

I was only mildly surprised. Jerry Gutman belonged to

the most uncanny subspecies in journalism, the city politics reporters. For Jerry, and his dozen or so colleagues who, like him, had mastered the recondite craft of reporting on New York municipal politics, the very stones of the city had tongues.

"You know I'm the careful type, Jerry," I said. "I don't talk before I write."

"Feeling independent?"

"As always."

"Ah, Skelton, the lone wolf!" His soft, nasal voice shifted into a W. C. Fields imitation. "Remember him well. Proud bugger. Too proud to accept the help of his friends. Works for a trade magazine in Philadelphia now, I believe."

"All right, all right," I said. "Are you free this afternoon?"

"I'll be free around five. You want to meet at The Lion's Head?"

"Fine. See you then."

The Lion's Head was a literary tavern on Christopher Street. It wasn't far from where I lived, and I arrived there exactly on the hour.

Jerry was standing at the bar, in the midst of a boisterous crowd of Irish journalists, poets, and bardic laborers, the hard-core habitués of the place. He extricated himself from the mob. "Let's go into the back room," he said, "where it's quieter." Dropping his voice, Jerry muttered, "That boozy Irish brilliance! All they do is make animal noises at each other!"

We sat at a table in a remote corner of the back room. A narrow rectangle of a window was above us. It offered a dog's-eye view of Sheridan Square. Pedestrian legs flashed by. Beyond, one could see the eroded little park in the center of the square.

Jerry put his pipe in his mouth and began the protracted process of lighting it. With the pipe and his neat, black, bolshevik-type beard, he looked like nothing so much as a slightly radical assistant professor of philosophy at Rutgers or City College.

The waitress came and we ordered our drinks. By then, Jerry had a decent coal glowing in the pipe bowl. He let out a mouthful of smoke and said, "So tell me all about Elliot Karp."

I stared at him. "You've got to be kidding!"

"Pardon?"

"I thought *you* had something to tell *me* about him."

"Me? I'm not investigating him. *You* are."

"For Christ's sake, Jerry," I burst out, annoyed, "what do you think I am? Your leg man? Go dig up your own material!"

"Don, Don," he gently chided, "that is not the attitude to take. I am not competing with you. If you've got a story, it's your story—*yours*—understand? We're not interested in Elliot Karp. We're interested in someone much more important."

"Like who?"

He seemed a bit surprised that I would ask. "The Mayor."

"Yeah? And who is this 'we'?"

"The good guys."

"I thought the Mayor was one of the good guys."

"That was last year."

I waited for him to go on. When he didn't, I said, "Okay, I'll bite. Who are the good guys this year?"

He looked pained. "Haven't you been reading my column?"

Jerry's column appeared in a hip, liberal weekly newspaper. He had his devoted readers but, the truth was, I wasn't one of them.

After a moment, I ventured, "Congressman Lampell?"

"That's right," he replied, rather wearily. "And, like any ordinarily well informed citizen, you know that Al Lampell is running against the Mayor in the primaries?"

"Yes, it so happens I *am* aware of that," I said. "So you're in with the Lampell people, huh?"

"He has my support."

"The Mayor has done some good things, hasn't he?"

"He's a nice man," Jerry said. "But he's a machine politician. And the time has come to break up the machine."

"Okay," I said. I didn't want to pursue it further. The twists and turns of fratricidal liberal politics were more than I could ever comprehend. "But what about Karp?" I asked. "If you're not going to do a piece on him, why do you need to know anything about him at all?"

"Because if I don't know what you've found out, I can't help you. And that's the whole point of this, Don, I want to *help*." He leaned forward and his tone became very earnest. "I want you to make good on this story. I want you to do a really terrific job. Not for your sake—though I think you're sweet—"

"For the sake of the good guys?"

"Well, it's obvious, isn't it? The worse you make Karp look, the better it is for us. A scandal in his inner circle is just about the last thing the Mayor needs with the primaries coming up. And, of course, it's exactly what we do need."

"Maybe I feel I can do this without your help, Jerry."

He shook his head. "This is my particular jungle," he said, "not yours. And you know what's likely to happen to someone who goes into a jungle without a trusty native guide? He ends up as bleached bones." He sucked on his pipe reflectively. "Or, to use a metaphor more appropriate to your situation, he could end up as nothing more than two gold fillings in a lye pit."

The image chilled me. "Karp is involved with the Mafia?"

"Could be. It's kind of standard for corrupt politicians in this town. I'll tell you *this,*" he said, pointing the stem of his pipe at me. "If you go around asking the wrong people the wrong questions, I don't want to be anywhere near you—on the street or in a slowly moving car."

"Are you trying to scare me with this talk?"

"I wouldn't dream of it. You're fearless." After a moment, he asked, "*Are* you scared?"

"A little," I admitted.

"Then accept my help." He put his hand over his heart. "I place my humble, obedient self at your service. If nothing else," he went on, "let's be practical about this. Something that might take you a year or never to find out, I can find out in one day."

Jerry was right, of course. I was a novice at political investigation. Jerry, on the other hand, had a fully developed network of contacts. There was someone he could go to in just about every municipal, state, and federal agency in the city.

"All right," I said. "I accept your kind offer."

"Good," Jerry said briskly. He took out a notebook and pencil. "Now, what have you got?"

"Maybe something, maybe nothing. I'm not sure." I told him exactly what Herndon had told me—that Karp, for some mysterious reason, had delayed a variance on a Broadway block front. Jerry scribbled furiously.

"One thing I don't understand," I said. "A variance is an exemption from a zoning restriction, right?"

"Right."

"Then why does Karp have any say on it? Isn't a variance decided upon by the Planning Commission?"

"Yeah," Jerry replied. "But the Agency for Urban Development is one of the Mayor's new superagencies. It has authority over the Planning Commission. And if Karp, as the director, refuses to give his approval to a variance, it stops it dead. So what else have you got?" he asked.

"Karp has been meeting with a mystery man," I said.

"What makes this mystery man so mysterious?"

"Well, he uses a phony name when he calls the office. 'Richard White.' His real first name is probably Gabe. Karp meets him in obscure Italian restaurants. He's short, fat, with gray hair. He has a high voice. He sounds like an angry old woman."

Jerry dutifully noted down these details. "Is that last vivid phrase yours?" he asked, as he wrote.

"That's the way my informant described him."

"And who's your informant?"

"Karp's secretary. His ex-secretary."

Jerry looked up at me, astonished. "Gwen? Gwen what's-her-name? You got to her? That's more than *I* could do."

"Sex appeal," I said airily. "Without it, you can't be the complete reporter."

"You son of a bitch," he murmured. His homely, bearded face clouded with something like envy. "Anything else?"

"That's it. That was all I could come up with." I shrugged. "It may not be much."

"It will do. Not bad for a rookie." He closed his notebook and put it away. "I'll check these out. Now, enough of these sordid matters." He downed his drink. "You want to go shoot some pool?"

"Sorry. I've got an appointment at six."

"Business?"

"In a way. A beautiful lady."

"You son of a bitch," he murmured again.

4 At a few minutes past six, I was indeed in the company of a very beautiful woman. We sat out on the terrace of her Upper East Side penthouse, having cocktails. The martinis were dry, the air was balmy, and it was strictly business. For the sake of my story, and even more for the sake of my peace of mind, I had come to find answers to some troubling questions.

"So Blake wants you to write an article on Elliot. How very strange!" Margrit Hivnor mused. She seemed to be studying the ribbon of traffic on the far shore of the river. In the twilight, it showed up as only a flow of headlights. That and the oily black of the river and the shadowy forms of some Queens factory buildings constituted her view. "Not a nice article, I suppose."

"All it has to be is accurate," I said.

She looked up at me now and smiled, a small, trained smile. "No, then it will not be nice."

Margrit's accent was lightly Swedish, with a faint overlay of British. She wasn't the conventional Scandinavian blonde; rather, she had chestnut hair and stark, dramatic features. In her heyday, she had been one of the top models. Her beauty had not diminished since then; it had simply become a more calculated thing. Her face was masklike; she barely moved a muscle in it when she spoke, smiled, or frowned. Her complexion, which was flawless anyway, was falsified by a slight excess of make-up, a sign that, even though she was not much past thirty, she already feared the onset of age.

"And Blake sent you to *me?* May I ask why?"

"Because you know Elliot so well."

"I am sure there are others who know him better."

"Not in the same way." I paused, then decided to be bold. "He is your lover, after all."

Her expression held its stillness. "That is not true."

"Perhaps I'm being too direct."

After a moment, she said, "He *was* my lover. No longer."

"It's over?"

"It is finished. Quite finished."

She took a sip of her martini; over the rim of the glass, her enormous dark eyes went on studying me. The light struck her in such a way that, beneath her filmy dress, I could discern the exact contours of her long, slender body. I suspected she was not unaware of this. "You must be very close to

Blake. *Very* close," she said, "if he has told you about Elliot and myself. Blake does not usually speak of it. It is very painful for him."

"I imagine it's painful for any husband."

Her penciled eyebrows arched perplexedly. "What is?"

"What you're talking about." Uncomfortably, I clarified. "Adultery."

"Adultery was not the issue." She seemed a bit surprised that I would bring up such an irrelevant point. "I had lovers before." She regarded me uncertainly for a moment. "If Blake has confided in you, then surely you know about the arrangement."

"I'm afraid I don't. What arrangement?"

"Perhaps you should ask Blake." A quiet, cold anger had come into her voice. "He tells you part of the story, I see—but not all of it? Has he become so hypocritical? Does he want to make people think I am some ordinary cheating housewife?"

"Blake told me very little," I said. "Maybe you should explain, just so I don't get the wrong idea."

She pursed her lips, debating whether or not she should tell me more than I knew already. Then she shrugged lightly, as if it were ultimately a matter of indifference to her. "Blake, as you know, is a masterful man," she said, her tone as icy and calm as ever. "He likes to control people. He likes to influence them. He likes to make choices for them. With me, this was true down to the smallest detail. This hair style," she said, touching her hair—"Blake selected it. This shade of lipstick—Blake selected it. And my lovers—" She let the sentence hang, unfinished.

"Blake selected them, too?"

"That would be an exaggeration. No, he did not select them. But he approved them—which is almost the same thing. That was part of our agreement, the agreement we made when we married. I told him then that I could never be faithful to him."

"Why did you feel that?"

Margrit smiled faintly, briefly, with the fleeting amusement that is inspired by a particularly stupid question. "Because I did not find Blake sexually interesting."

"And so you worked out this arrangement?"

"Yes. Blake gave me my freedom. In return, I recounted to him, in great detail, everything I did with that freedom. Sometimes this would excite him very much." A weary contempt crept into her voice. "There seems to be something of the voyeur in all you journalists."

There was no hint of guilt, no touch of embarrassment in Margrit's manner. She had the pride of the courtesan; she was not to be judged by the standards one applies to the common run of females.

"And Elliot was one of these approved lovers?" I asked.

"No, he was not. Blake did not know about him. He did not find out until very late."

"Why did you keep it a secret?"

She considered the question for a moment. "I suppose I wanted to have something of my own. Something I would not have to share with Blake. And, with Elliot—well—" she shrugged—"it was different."

"What made it different?"

"I think I was a little in love with him."

"Elliot was special, huh? Not like the other men?"

"No, he was not like the other men." She regarded me coolly, as if she had detected something unsympathetic in my tone and was trying to assess it. "Elliot is a good man," she said. "He is a kind man. And he is a romantic." With a wry smile, she added, "I am susceptible to romantics."

"Was he in love with you?"

"That is hard to say. He was drawn to me—as I was drawn to him. Mutual need, perhaps, since he, too, is an alien."

"He's a native-born American," I corrected her.

She shook her head. "He is an alien *here*—in this New

York world." She paused. "No, that is not quite what I mean. Elliot would be an alien—" she gestured helplessly, momentarily inarticulate—*"anywhere.* There can be no home for a man like that, you know?"

"No, I don't know. But then, I'm not a romantic. I'm just a guy writing a piece on a politician."

"Yes, of course." Margrit put aside her glass and leaned back a little in her deck chair. "Now, may I ask you a question?"

"Go ahead."

"What does Blake mean by sending you to me? Does he really expect you to write about all this in his magazine?"

"No." I had dissembled long enough. It was time to set things right. "Blake didn't send me here. I came here on my own. In fact, Blake has never talked to me at all about your affair with Elliot."

"I see," she said, after a moment. "Then you are a very deceitful man."

"Maybe. But I felt I had to do it. There was something I had to find out."

"What?"

"I needed to know why Blake wants me to write this piece."

"It will be an unflattering piece?"

"Yes. Very unflattering."

"Then the answer is obvious," she said. "Blake hates Elliot. He hates him because, for a time, Elliot was more important to me than he was. Blake is a supreme egotist. He could forgive many things, but never that. I had loved another man, I had kept it a secret from him." She shrugged. "And that was it. I had broken our agreement. So our marriage was finished." With a faintly mocking smile, she asked, "Now, does that make you feel any better? To know why you have been hired to destroy Elliot?"

"It doesn't make much difference either way," I said. "It's a job."

She laughed shortly. "And I thought *I* was the most cynical person I knew."

"Maybe Elliot is. He happens to be a very corrupt politician."

"I imagine he is." Her tone was unsurprised and unimpressed. She rose. "I have a dinner engagement. I must get ready."

"Of course." I rose also.

We went back inside. Margrit walked me to the front door. When I paused to say good-by, she said, "I wish you luck with your project."

"Thanks. Oh, by the way," I asked, "you wouldn't happen to know a certain acquaintance of Elliot's? A man named Gabe? Or Richard White?"

"No," she said, "those names mean nothing to me."

"Didn't think they would. Well, thanks again." I started to open the door.

"Mr. Skelton—"

I looked at her. "Yeah?"

"Elliot takes trips outside the country. Frequently." Her face was totally expressionless. "He never says what he does on those trips."

I waited for her to continue. "Go on. What else?"

"That is all. I thought you should know."

Suddenly the mask crumbled. For one instant her face registered anguish. She bit her lip and turned away abruptly. She moved off to the center of the room and stood with her back to me.

"You didn't have to tell me that," I said. "Why did you?"

"Because, as I said, the affair is finished." Her voice was flat and bitter.

"Were you the one who ended it?"

"Elliot did." She turned to me. Her mask was whole again, placid, but, behind it, I sensed her anger and humiliation. "That never happened to me before—a lover telling *me* it was over."

"Why did he?"

"Elliot loves his wife. The poor romantic fool loves his wife very much." Margrit's smile was faintly incredulous. "That may be so. But then, why should *I* protect him?"

six

1 A couple of nights later, Jerry Gutman and I met again at The Lion's Head.

We sat at the same corner table in the back room, which, since it was late evening, was quite crowded. Some NYU students were at the next table, a dating couple was opposite, and, in the center of the room, a merry Greenwich Village Irishman was setting his table aroar with every other thing he said.

Jerry surveyed the scene as he lit his pipe, then took out his notebook. "I've got a few little goodies for you."

"You work fast," I said, impressed. "Was it much trouble?"

"No trouble at all, m'boy," he said, lapsing into his W. C. Fields imitation. "A trifling task. Hardly a fit challenge for my cogitative faculties." He opened the notebook and squinted at a page. "Ah, yes-s-s." In his own voice, he said, "The variance on Broadway."

"Yeah, what about it?"

"It's just like you said. Karp has stalled a variance. That particular variance would permit a new office building to go up on Broadway in the Forties. Now, this project would seem to be a definite plus in that blighted area. Who would be opposed? A massage parlor, a porno bookstore, and a few other tawdry business establishments would be evicted. But, other than those folks, everyone should be happy about it, right?"

"All right," I asked patiently, "who *is* opposed?"

"Well, it so happens that another office building went up on the next block just a couple of years ago, and it's still only half occupied. Obviously, this new building would represent very damaging competition."

"Who owns that building on the next block?"

"An outfit called Stonetown Enterprises. Don't be misled by the flinty New England sound of that name. It's a front business for Aladino Gero."

"The gangster?"

Jerry winced. "Bite your tongue when you say that. Aladino Gero is no mere hoodlum. He's head of one of The Five Families. A very distinguished character. An elder statesman. The Disraeli of the Cosa Nostra."

"And you think Karp may be hooked up with Gero?"

"If I had only this to go on, I'd say it *might* be a coincidence. But then there's this mysterious Gabe who calls himself 'Richard White.'" He sucked on his pipe thoughtfully. "One of the top capos in the Gero family," he went on, "is named Gabriele Podesta—or just plain Gabe to his friends. Podesta is Gero's go-between in his dealings with the politicians he has on his payroll—judges and other such honest employees. Gabe Podesta fits the description you gave me— short, fat, and gray-haired. And he does have a high voice. I know, I've talked with him on the phone a couple of times."

"Gabe Podesta," I repeated. "That sounds familiar. What does he do? Does he have a legit business?"

"By profession, he's a lawyer. Mainly, he's a real-estate operator. He owns a dozen or so buildings, some of them gained by dubious means. And he runs a couple of gay bars down here."

"Here in the Village?"

"Sure. The Village is his turf. His office is only a couple of blocks away."

I remembered now that the *Times* had published an exposé on the gay bars in the Village, and in it Gabe Podesta had been named as the owner of the two most notorious dives.

"You've got me convinced," I said. "It has to be the man." With satisfaction, I realized that at last I had it, the incriminating connection. I now had a hook in Elliot Karp. "Tell me about the Gero family. Haven't they been going around killing people?"

"Yes. But only their own kind," Jerry pointed out reasonably. "And Gero has lost a few men, too. There's a small war going on in the Mafia."

"What's the dispute?"

"Drugs."

Jerry was about to continue, but at that moment the Irishman at the center table broke into song, an unsteady, bass-voiced rendition of "The Mountains of Morne." Jerry waited, flinching slightly at each off-pitch high note, until the man finished—fortunately, he sang only one verse—and the delirious applause at the center table died down.

"About ten years ago," Jerry went on, "the Mafia got out of the drug trade. There had been some big arrests and they decided it wasn't worth it. But Aladino Gero, elderly gent though he is, thinks young and thinks big. And he's got a nice, healthy power drive. He thinks it's a damned shame the South Americans are making all that loot when there's so much local talent going to waste, and now he wants to take over. But he knows he can't do it the old way. The Turkey-to-Marseilles

French connection is too risky now. It's obsolete. So Gero is trying to develop a new Asian route."

"And I gather some of the other Mafia families disagree with Gero?"

"Vehemently."

"How's the war going?"

"Hard to say," Jerry replied, with a shrug. "Gero seems to be getting the best of it. But I don't know the exact body count as of now." He glanced at his pipe bowl. The coal had gone out. "If I'm telling you all this, it's to make a point."

"What's the point?"

"Be careful," he said gently. "You're not fooling around with press agents and producers now. You're getting in with some very heavy people."

"I never take unnecessary risks."

"You already have." He tapped the pipe empty and put it away. "I'm the craven type, myself. I try never to get involved in these things. But I'm fond of you, Don, and I'd kind of miss you if you weren't around any more." He regarded me for a moment, rather placidly. He seemed more intrigued by my danger than concerned by it. "If you get into real trouble, let me know. I'll do what I can."

I felt slightly chilled. But, nonchalantly enough, I said, "Thanks, Jerry."

"And if I *can't* do anything—" he smiled benevolently—"I'll write you one hell of a memorial column."

2 The phone rang as I was getting out of the shower. I gave myself a hasty once-over with a towel, hurried into the bedroom, and picked up the receiver.

"Don? Chico Melendez here."

"Chico! How are you?"

"Pretty good, man. I'm going to be working with you. Your Penelope Wren piece."

"That's terrific!" I was genuinely pleased. Chico was one of the best photographers in the business, and we had always worked well together.

"I'm shooting some pictures of Penelope Wren at her place tomorrow morning," Chico said. "Blake thinks you should be there. Can you make it?"

"Sure." I paused. I had to be careful with Chico. I assumed he didn't know the real purpose of the article. "Will this be the only session?"

"Blake didn't say."

"I'd like to get some pictures of her with her husband."

"Not tomorrow. He's out of town."

I was suddenly alert. "Where'd he go?"

"I don't know." He sounded a bit taken aback by my tone. "Wait a minute," he said after a moment, "I remember. He's gone to Brazil. Rio, I think they said."

"What's he doing in Rio?"

"How the hell would I know?"

"Never mind." I quickly changed the subject. "What time is the call tomorrow?"

"Eleven. I'll pick you up, if you want."

"Okay, fine."

As I dressed, I pondered the meaning of Karp's sudden trip to Brazil. It could have no sinister meaning at all. There were financiers who made such trips as a matter of course. But Elliot Karp, as I had discovered, was no financial whiz kid. In fact, the only going capitalist concern he seemed to be involved with was Aladino Gero's Mafia family.

I hadn't forgotten Margrit Hivnor's pointed reference to Karp's mysterious trips outside the country. In my thoughts, I had returned to it again and again. But I hadn't been able to figure out the significance of these trips. Then Jerry Gutman had told me of Gero's ambition to create a new route for smuggling heroin from Asia, and suddenly I had seen a possible connection. A wild surmise, perhaps; but now, with this quick trip to Brazil, the supposition didn't seem quite so farfetched.

I had carried out some research and had learned that 90 per cent of the illegal heroin in the U.S. now originated in the Golden Triangle, the remote opium-poppy growing area that lies at the juncture of Burma, Laos, and Thailand. On the traditional route, the morphine base flowed through the Middle East to Marseilles, where it was refined into heroin and then sent on to the U.S. The governments involved had succeeded in partly choking off this route. So a new route had evolved. It traversed Africa and crossed the ocean to South America. The heroin might arrive at any large port of entry —Rio de Janeiro, for instance.

This route was presently in the hands of independent South American entrepreneurs. The heroin was smuggled into the U.S. piecemeal by hundreds of Cubans and other Miami-based Latin Americans, who would bring the stuff in, one or two ounces at a time. Organized crime on the Mafia scale had yet to lay claim to this traffic; but now, according to Jerry, Aladino Gero was making his move.

Suppose such a Mafia project existed and Karp was involved in it—what would his function be? He would, of course, be invaluable to an international heroin ring. As one of the highest-ranking public officials in New York City, he was beyond suspicion and immune to search. But would he be some kind of liaison man? Or would he himself be engaged in smuggling?

Well, this was all conjecture. I had nothing tangible, no shred of evidence.

By the time I was through dressing, it was ten minutes to nine. I had dawdled, and, it suddenly occurred to me, I had given the morning-paper thief a chance to strike. This culprit, whoever he was, passed by my house at a quarter to nine. Or I assumed he did; unless I retrieved my copy of the *Times* from the doorstep by that time, it would usually be gone.

I hurried out of the apartment and down the stairs. A man was in the vestibule. He looked too straight and respectable in his dark-blue suit to be the thief, and obviously he had other business. He was bending over the mailboxes, studying the names.

"Looking for someone?"

He peered at me uncertainly. "You, I think." He was young, about my age, with curly hair, thin lips, and somber, dark eyes. "Are you Mr. Skelton?"

"Yes, I am."

"My name is Zanelli. I'm an assistant U.S. attorney." He didn't offer his hand.

"Am I in some kind of trouble?"

His silence left open the possibility that I was.

"Excuse me," I said. I brushed past him and opened the outside door. As I had expected, my *Times* was gone. "I have a case for you," I said, turning back to Zanelli. "Someone just stole my paper." This didn't elicit even the hint of a smile. "Or does it have to cross a state line?" I asked.

My wit was wasted on him—it usually is with law-enforcement people. "May I step inside so we can talk for a minute?" His accent was Lower East Side or Brooklyn. But he had a prosecutor's cold politesse.

"Sure." I pushed open the door to the hall. Zanelli went in. Then he stepped back, waiting for me to go up the stairs first. I didn't imagine I looked like the type who would pounce on a man from behind. But Zanelli evidently took no chances.

When Zanelli entered the living room, he moved to the exact center of it and stood, clear of everything. It was as if he were so grimly official that he was unwilling to relate to anything so personal as a piece of my furniture.

Uneasily, I waited for him to say something, anything, that would reveal the intent of his visit. Finally, I asked, "So what's the trouble?"

"There won't be any trouble," he said, "if you're reasonable."

"I always try to be reasonable, Mr. Zanelli."

Zanelli looked around. His head moved in forty-five-degree arcs, pausing briefly in between, as if there were a camera behind his eyes snapping pictures. He held longest on the fraction of my study he could see through the open doorway. A few steps forward and he could have taken in the whole of it. But he stood where he was, scrupulously avoiding the appearance of a search without a warrant. "You write about show-business people, don't you?"

"That's my special area, yes."

He turned and faced me. "Why don't you stay with it?"

"I don't understand. What do you mean?"

"Stay with it," he said. "Stay with what you know."

"That's just what I'm doing." I could hear the nervousness in my voice; I knew I had to be careful. It was safest to play it straight—the honest, misunderstood entertainment writer. "Right now, for instance," I said, "I'm writing a piece on a movie actress. Penelope Wren—I don't know if you've heard of her."

He nodded. "Mrs. Karp."

"That's right," I said, with a proper touch of astonishment. "Her married name *is* Karp."

"And you're not interested in *Mr.* Karp at all?"

"Interested in him?" I laughed. "God, no! I've met him. He's a pompous young windbag. But then," I added, "I find most politicians boring. I'm apolitical, you know."

"I'm glad to hear that." He came close to a smile; it was a twitch of his mouth that was like the quick bending of a knife. "In that case, you'll have no reason to put more than one or two lines about Mr. Karp in your article."

This stopped me for a moment. I was up against something new and unexpected, something that seemed incomprehensible. Why would the Justice Department want to protect a corrupt municipal politician? "Does the U.S. Attorney's office frequently provide editorial advice?"

"When we have to."

I feigned an innocent perplexity. "You're worried that if I put in more than, let's say, one or two lines about Elliot Karp, I'll distort the focus of my piece?"

"We're not worried. You're the one who should worry." His voice got very hard. "Because if you write more than a bare, flattering mention of Elliot Karp, you're going to be in worse trouble than you've ever dreamed of."

"Is this a threat, Mr. Zanelli?"

He considered the question. "Yes," he said. "It's a threat."

I moved away, trying to collect my thoughts. I started to sit, then decided against it. Somehow I couldn't make myself that comfortable, not with Zanelli standing, stiff as a hangman, in the center of my living-room floor.

I felt confused; the whole thing had become crazily reversed. In my journalistic righteousness, it had never occurred to me that I might be seen as the criminal, I might be the one threatened by the law.

Well, perhaps it was a misunderstanding. Perhaps Zanelli was under the impression that I was hounding an innocent public official.

"What if I have a story?" I asked. "A story about corruption in very high places?"

"Do you have evidence of such corruption?"

"Let's say I did."

"Then you should turn over the evidence to us. This kind of investigation is our job, not yours."

"But you're the federal government."

"There is a federal statute that applies to corruption within municipal administrations."

"Oh, is there? I haven't noticed you doing too much about it."

His chilly near-smile flickered again. "We're getting better," he said.

"But what about the public's right to know?" I asked.

"That's journalist's cant. The law recognizes no such right."

"Have you heard of the First Amendment, by any chance?"

"Freedom of speech. That's something quite different."

"All right, then," I said. "Maybe I feel like exercising my freedom of speech."

He regarded me impassively. "Your tax forms may be looked at more closely," he said.

"They won't find a thing," I said. "My tax forms are painfully honest."

"Charitable contributions?"

"I don't list any. I'm a hardhearted bastard."

He was silent for a moment. Then, almost gently, he said, "You realize, of course, that a court order can require you to reveal the sources of your information. Are you prepared to do so?"

"Of course I'm not."

"Then you'll stay in jail until you do."

I felt a chill of apprehension. This was no empty threat, I knew. One journalist of my acquaintance had rotted away in a county jail throughout the life of a grand jury. As a result of a new Supreme Court ruling, it was happening all over the country. The ultimate intimidation of the press.

"You know, Mr. Zanelli," I said, "it's lucky that I'm so good-natured and apolitical. If I were someone else, I might call you a fascist."

Zanelli's eyes flared for an instant. Then he turned abruptly and crossed to the door. I thought he was about to make an angry, wordless exit. But, instead, he faced me again, as self-collected and emotionless as ever.

"What do you want, Mr. Skelton?" he asked. "Some snappy copy for your readers, isn't that it? This is just a job to you—like a hundred other jobs you've done?" His tone was mild and reasonable; he was now the common-sensical family lawyer. "You can write something very nice about Mrs. Karp, something very colorful, and your readers will be happy. But if you overreach yourself, if you try to interfere in this *other* area— well, you just don't know what you're doing. And, if you don't know what you're doing, someone might get hurt. *You* might get hurt. And we don't want anyone to get hurt," he concluded quietly. "I'm sure you're a sensible man, Mr. Skelton. Please, think about it."

After Zanelli left, I did, in fact, spend the better part of an hour thinking about it. But I didn't ponder the rightness of my course of action. Rather, I tried to figure out the reason for this peculiar visitation. Zanelli, presumably speaking for the U.S. Attorney's office, had made a somewhat crude but forthright attempt to scare me off. Why? Was I trespassing on some investigation that was already under way?

It was possible—and yet how had Zanelli known? It hadn't surprised me that Jerry Gutman had caught wind of what I was up to. The inner circle of journalists was a small, incestuous group, and if Blake Hivnor, or one of his assistants, had dropped an incautious word about my assignment, it would soon have reached Jerry's ears. But a federal bureaucrat was something else. To the best of my knowledge, the U.S. Attorney's office was not tuned in to our particular closed circuit.

If Zanelli knew, it could only be because someone had gone out of his way to tell him, someone who had grown suspicious of me. The more I thought about it, the more it seemed likely that it was Elliot Karp himself.

In that case, could Zanelli be an accomplice of Karp's? And, if so, did the conspiracy extend beyond Zanelli to still higher ranking individuals? Could so august a personage as the U.S. Attorney be involved? At what point did the corruption stop?

This speculation was slightly dizzying. I was an honest provincial, raised to respect the laws and the elected representatives of my democracy. But now I felt disoriented; I found myself in a cold, hostile landscape where there was no true light or true dark, where nothing was what it seemed, where the law was but one more ruse and the leaders were the most slithery, dangerous predators of all.

It was a terrifying vision, and I tried to reject it. It was paranoia, I told myself; I should wait until I had the facts.

And yet, as I sat in my living room that gray morning, I felt very alone and rather fearful. I was a professional; I made good on all my assignments, and this one, too, I would stick with to the end. I would search out the truth.

But there were some truths, if they existed, that I would rather not know.

3 The next morning, Chico Melendez came by to pick me up. He didn't bother ringing the bell. Instead, he honked his horn three times, sharply.

I hurried down the stairs and out onto the sidewalk. Chico's battered Mercury, its engine idling, was parked square in front of my steps. "Hey, Don!" Chico intoned, raising his hand out of the open car window in a grave salute. His smile of greeting, if it was there at all, was hidden by his drooping black mustache.

"How are you, Chico?"

"Dead beat, man," he replied.

"Working too hard?"

"Balling," he said mournfully. "Guess I'm getting old."

I got into the car. Chico eased the Mercury forward. At the intersection, he turned up the avenue slowly and smoothly, careful not to jiggle the cameras and collapsible lights in the leather bags on the back seat.

Chico didn't say anything as he drove; he simply hummed an indistinct tune under his breath. In his work clothes and sandals, he seemed like some amiable Mexican laborer, tooling about in a junky old car. Actually, he was a highly paid photographer, who had photographed all of the most beautiful women in New York. This was a routine morning's work for him.

At length, I asked, "Have you ever photographed Penelope Wren before?"

"Sure. A few years back. I did a spread on her for *Vogue.*"

"What did you think of her?"

"One of the best," he said. "Great bone structure."

"What did you think of her as a person?"

He gave me a brief, askance look. "She was a model, man. Not a person."

We arrived at the Karps' address. While Chico got his equipment out of the back of the car, I went up the steps of the brownstone and rang the bell. The maid, a stout German woman, opened the door. She gazed at me blankly. She had seen me before, at the Karps' cocktail party, but now she showed no recognition. "What do you want?" she asked.

"We're here to photograph Mrs. Karp," I said.

"Mrs. Karp is not here."

"Mrs. Karp knows about this," I explained patiently. "It's all been arranged. Pictures for the article in *View* magazine?"

"Mrs. Karp is not here," the maid repeated. "She has gone out."

"She's gone out!" I stared at the maid, astonished. "Did she forget?"

"No, she did not forget. Something has happened."

"What's happened?"

"There was a phone call. Then she went out. That is all I know."

"When did she leave?"

"A few minutes ago."

"Did Mrs. Karp seem upset?"

The maid's eyes narrowed. She was naturally suspicious of strangers who asked personal questions. *"Ja,* she was upset."

"Where is she now?"

"I cannot tell you that." Sternly, she added, "You must not bother her."

"I don't want to bother her. I just want to call and leave a message." The maid maintained a stolid silence. "Please, miss," I pleaded. "We went to all the trouble of coming up here."

She scowled uncertainly for another moment, then relented. "She is at her father's house," she said. She swung the door shut in my face.

Chico was coming up the steps, his leather bags slung over his shoulder. "What's the deal?" he asked.

"The session's off."

"What the hell is this?" He stopped on a middle step, suddenly irate. "I've wasted an hour!"

"Discuss it with Blake," I said. "I'm just a hired hand, myself." I took out my notebook and flipped through it. I had made a point of getting James Wren's home address from Tod Cushman. This was standard operating procedure for me—to get the home phone numbers and addresses of everyone involved in a story. I never knew when I might have to make a house call.

I found the address. Wren lived only a few blocks away. "Chico, would you do me a favor?" I asked. "On the way back, could you drop me off at Sixty-eighth Street?"

Five minutes later, Chico let me off in front of James Wren's town house, a stately, five-story gray stone. It was that New York rarity, an old private home that had been left intact. The door was slightly ajar, as if someone had been careless or had made a hasty, excited entrance into the house.

I rang the doorbell, which trilled resoundingly within the

depths of the house. I waited for what might have been a full
minute, but no one came to the door.

Then, suddenly, I heard a man cry out in a muffled, indistinct voice that seemed to come from a closed upper room of the
house, a string of blurred-together words, perhaps two sentences
in all. It was a deep voice, but it had the petulant, injured note
of a put-upon child. Another male voice cut in and overlapped
it, higher pitched, quieter, hypercalm.

The house was silent again. I stood there uncertainly for a
moment, then pushed open the door. A flight of stairs rose before me. Voices again, this time a quiet, impersonal voice and a
woman's voice—Penelope's, I assumed; they seemed to be coming from a room just off the second-floor landing.

I climbed the stairway and came to a stop outside the
closed door of the room. I could hear what was being said now.

"He'll be asleep in a moment," the calm man was saying.
"Would you get some fresh linen, please? Ernest can remake
the bed."

"Won't it disturb him?" Penelope asked.

"I've given him a stiff injection. When he's out, he'll stay
out."

"I'll be right back," Penelope said.

The door opened. Penelope appeared in the doorway. She
froze when she saw me. "What are you doing here?" she whispered angrily.

Penelope, unthinking in her shock, left the door open for
about three seconds. It was long enough for me to take in the
room, to catch the image of James Wren on the bed, with the
doctor and Ernest, his manservant, on either side of him.

Wren lay on his back, naked, a blood-splattered sheet
covering him to the waist. His mouth was hanging open and his
eyes were almost closed. His head was shaved—imperfectly,
as if he had done the job himself; small tufts of white hair
spotted his scraped skull. There were several long cuts, the kind

that might be made if one slashed at one's head with a dull razor. The more shallow lacerations had been merely swabbed with a purplish antiseptic. Two deeper wounds had bandages taped over them.

The doctor was checking Wren's pulse rate as he sank into unconsciousness. Ernest, his face damp with sweat, was looking down numbly at his prostrate employer. There were bloodstains on his clothes, widely dispersed over his white shirt and black trousers, as if he had thrown his whole body into a struggle with a copiously bleeding man.

Penelope closed the door. Her voice soft and cold, she asked again, "What are you doing here?"

I was too shaken by what I had just seen to answer at once. I took a moment to collect myself, then said, "You weren't there for the picture session. I wanted to know what was wrong. I'm sorry. If I'd realized it was something like this—"

"Now you know," she said curtly. "Please, leave."

"Is there anything I can do to help?"

"There is absolutely *nothing* you can do."

"I'd like to talk with you for a moment."

"What?" She stared at me in amazement. "Don't you see? I can't talk with anybody now! Get out!"

"I'm sorry, Penelope, but I can't leave," I said quietly, "not until I understand what's going on."

Penelope gazed at me helplessly. She was in no mental state to argue with me; I could sense her tightly withheld hysteria. She glanced back over her shoulder at the door of the room, as if she were about to call for help. But she caught herself. Even in her distraught condition, she realized it would be wiser not to make a scene of it.

"Come with me," she said. She walked away down the hall and opened the door of the room at the very end. "Wait in here."

I stepped into the room. Penelope closed the door after me. I heard her footsteps recede down the hall.

I looked around. The room was fully furnished, right down to the small, expensive details: antique jade inkpots on the writing desk, a set of ivory combs on the dressing table. But there was a mustiness; the air felt dead. I guessed that no one had actually lived in this room for quite a long time. The toy panda that sat spread-legged on the bed looked mournful and neglected. Its crown was gray with dust.

I heard the doctor's voice at the other end of the hall. I opened the door a few inches and peered out. The doctor, satchel in hand, was emerging from Wren's bedroom.

I went out of the room and walked briskly down the hall toward the doctor. He stopped and regarded me curiously. "Hello," he said.

"Hello." I thrust out my hand. "I'm Don Skelton. I'm a friend of the family."

He shook my hand. "Glad to meet you." He was about Wren's age, ruddy-cheeked and professionally genial. His smile seemed almost inappropriately cheery. "Penny called you?"

I nodded. "In case I was needed. Will the Senator be all right?"

"Oh, certainly. The lacerations are superficial. They'll be all healed in a few days."

"Is this as bad as last time?"

"Last time?" he echoed.

"In July, or whenever it was. You were the doctor then, weren't you?"

"Yes, I was." He considered my question for a moment. "It's as bad," he said. "It's worse, in fact. This time, Jim is going to have to go into a sanitarium. For his own protection. Before he hurts himself more seriously." He eyed me quizzically. "Skelton? I don't think Jim has mentioned you."

"Well, the Senator has many friends," I said.

He smiled again, rather uncertainly now. "Tell Penny I'll be waiting in the living room," he said. He went down the stairs.

I didn't linger to relay the message, but quickly returned to the room, closed the door, and stood just on the other side of it, listening at the crack.

I could hear Penelope's footsteps as she came back and went into her father's room. Thirty seconds later, the door opened again. Penelope came out and went down the stairs to the ground floor.

I relaxed and lit a cigarette; Penelope would be in the living room awhile, talking with the doctor. I went over to the dressing table and studied the two framed photographs on it. One showed Penelope as a gawky, smiling, teen-age girl, her arm around the waist of an equally gawky, smiling, teen-age boy. The other photograph showed the young James Wren kneeling beside a little girl of three or four, who was just barely recognizable as Penelope.

Wren was smiling at his daughter joyfully. At this point, he was, I calculated, a congressman beginning his political career, the darling of the liberal wing of his party. His prime years lay ahead of him. The tanned, firm-jawed, handsome face was supremely confident. There was no awareness in it that there could be such an end point as financial ruin. Or madness.

The little girl, in contrast, was serious-faced. Her large, luminous eyes were solemn, almost haunted. As very young children sometimes do, she seemed to carry a premonition of tragedy.

The door opened behind me. I turned quickly. Penelope stood in the doorway, gazing at me. I stepped away from the photographs. I felt suddenly uneasy, guilty, as if I had been caught trifling with sacred relics.

Penelope walked directly to the dressing table and looked down at the long-ago photograph of her father and herself. "I love this picture," she said. "Daddy looks so happy." Her voice was very soft, almost dreamy. Only her hands betrayed her inner agitation. They clutched at each other convulsively. She looked at me and, very politely, asked, "Is there anything else you want to see? I have some old love letters in that desk drawer. Would you like to read through them?"

"That won't be necessary," I said uncomfortably.

"Look around." She spoke more rapidly now, with a strained edginess in her voice. "I spent twenty-one years of my life here. Ask me about anything. My panda?" She gestured toward the stuffed toy animal on the bed. "You want to know his name? Miles. My dresses?" She went to the closet and threw open the door. "Look, they're all still here. Daddy has kept them. And there are costumes, too, see? Little Chinese girl?" —she touched a faded gold-embroidered gown—"Spanish dancer?"—and then a black lace dress. "I'd put these on and do my little dances and my little songs for Daddy and he'd laugh and clap and call me his darling, his miracle, the most beautiful girl in the world. Where's your notebook, Don? Why aren't you taking all this down?"

"I'm sorry," I murmured. "I shouldn't have stayed." I took a step to go.

"It doesn't make any difference now." She sat on the bed and stared before her. In a flat, drained voice, she asked, "What do you want to know?"

She had succeeded in shaming me and I really didn't have the heart for any more questions. But still, I had a job to do. "How long has your father been mentally ill?" I asked.

"Daddy has been—subject to depressions—for some time." She spoke slowly, choosing her words painfully. "Recently, it's gotten worse. Most of the time, he's all right. He functions. He goes to his office—"

"—and answers letters written ten years ago." Penelope looked at me guardedly, then nodded slightly. "What happens to those letters he writes?" I asked. "Does Ernest destroy them?"

"No. Ernest puts them in a box. I don't know why—" she gestured vaguely—"but we feel we should save them."

"What will happen now? You'll report this as another

'mild heart attack'? And the Senator will be sent off to some quiet place in the country?"

"Yes."

"And then what?"

"Daddy will get better." She said it with the simple faith of a child. "He's been under terrible pressure these last few years. But he'll get better. I know he will."

"Well, I hope so, too."

Penelope was silent. She drifted off into some private reverie. Abstractedly, she reached for the toy panda and took it into her arms. She hugged it to her chest.

"I guess I'll be going," I said. I crossed to the door. "I'm really sorry, Penelope. And I'm sorry I disturbed you at such an unfortunate time."

"Maybe it's just as well." She hadn't moved. Sitting on the edge of the bed, clutching her panda, she seemed not the poised, stately beauty, but, rather, the undefined little girl, fragile, vulnerable, frightened. "Because now you've seen it for yourself. And you know what you'll be doing to my father if you write that story."

"I don't intend to write anything at all about your father."

"No, but you're going to write about Elliot. You're going to do a hatchet job on him." Her voice was toneless, dead. "You're going to expose those silly little lies he told about his past, and you're going to make him seem ridiculous—isn't that so? And the humiliation of it will destroy my father. It will be the last crushing blow. After that, Daddy will never get any better."

"Penelope—" I hesitated. I knew I didn't have to justify myself. But, at the same time, I couldn't go away and leave that accusing stare unanswered. "It's not simply a matter of a few lies. There's much more than that."

"There's nothing else," she said. She cuddled the panda, pressing its fuzzy, dusty cheek against her own.

"I know you'll have a hard time accepting this." I paused, then went ahead and said it, as directly as I could. "Elliot is a totally unprincipled man. He took advantage of your father's mental condition to gain control over him. And then he used your father every way he could—to get ahead in business and to get ahead in politics." Penelope didn't react; she didn't even look at me. I couldn't be sure she actually heard what I was saying. "I've learned some pretty scary things about Elliot," I went on. "The kinds of things that just can't be overlooked. He's a very dangerous man, Penelope. He's a danger to you —to your father—to everyone in this city."

Penelope was staring at some point on the carpet between us. Her eyes were blank. "That's not true," she whispered. "None of it is."

"My God," I burst out, "how can I make you see it? Elliot is a criminal! He associates with criminals! He is involved in the most sordid evil activities!"

She looked up at me quickly. "I don't want to see you again," she said.

It was hopeless, I realized. She was sealed off from me; there was no way I could reach her. It was foolish of me even to have made the attempt. But I couldn't undo it, and there was nothing I could say now that would erase the naked hostility in her eyes.

"All right," I said, with a shrug. "I tried." I turned and opened the door. "Good-by." I looked back at her for one last time.

A smile had come to Penelope's lips. It was oddly like that of the panda in her arms, the empty, unfelt smile of a toy. "I'm going to do everything I can to stop you," she said. "You'll never publish that story."

seven

1 The limousine was first in line, parked directly in front of the glass doors of the Arrivals Terminal. Chico and I were three cars back, sitting in the old Mercury. The windows were open, but it was a warm day and we were damp and uncomfortable.

Chico tapped his fingers impatiently on the steering wheel. He was getting restive. "How do you know he's on this flight?" he asked.

"I checked with his office," I said. "I double-checked. Have faith in me."

"Yeah, sure," he muttered grumpily. "I'm blowing a whole afternoon and you tell me to have faith!"

"It won't be long now. At least, the plane was on time."

"He could be in there another half hour."

"He'll be the first one out. They'll whisk him through customs."

Within seconds, I was proved right. The glass doors slid

open and Elliot Karp, dispatch case in hand, emerged and walked briskly over to the limousine. A Pan Am official was one step behind, carrying Karp's suitcase. The chauffeur got out of the limousine and took the suitcase. Karp paused to chat for a moment with the eagerly smiling Pan Am man. He had not relinquished the dispatch case.

"He travels light," I said. "One suitcase and a dispatch case. What's in that dispatch case, I wonder?"

"Papers," Chico said. "And more papers. What makes you so sure he's got dope on him?"

"I'm *not* sure," I replied. "But if he is smuggling the stuff, this next hour is the time to deliver it. When you're between the airport and home, you're in limbo. You're not where you were and you haven't arrived yet. You're out of touch with the world. No one knows exactly where you are."

"That's profound, you know?" Chico put on his reverential peon expression. "That's why it gives me such a big thrill to hang around with you writers. Deep thinkers!"

Karp had gotten into the rear of the limousine. The sleek, black vehicle pulled away from the curb.

"Come on," I said. "Let's go."

Chico started the car. We followed the limousine to the Long Island Expressway. The limousine eased into the Manhattan-bound stream of traffic. Chico let a car pass, then darted in behind. Screened by the intervening car, we tailed the limousine. The traffic was reasonably calm, and, as the Queens landmarks slid by—Lefrak City, the World's Fair dome—our particular linkage in the line of cars held firm. When we arrived at the Midtown Tunnel, we were still two cars behind the limousine.

Emerging from the tunnel, the limousine took the uptown, right turn.

"Well, he's not going to his office, anyway," I commented.

"No, of course not," Chico said. "He's going home. To take a shower and freshen up. What else?"

"Maybe. We'll see."

We proceeded up Third Avenue. In the Forties, we were snagged suddenly by a red light; the limousine went on and grew dangerously distant. When the light changed, Chico accelerated to catch up. As we sped up the avenue, narrowing the gap again, the potholes in the crumbling surface jolted the Mercury and bounced us around. Ahead of us, the stately limousine passed over each pit in the pavement with barely a shudder.

As the limousine approached Seventy-second Street, it slowed down and pulled over to the curb.

I was suddenly alert. "Hey, what's this?"

"Sorry, man," Chico said. "Got to keep going."

We cruised by the limousine. At the intersection, the light turned red and we came to a stop. I twisted around in my seat to see what was happening.

Karp and the chauffeur got out. The chauffeur held the front door open and Karp slid into the driver's seat. The chauffeur slammed the door shut. The limousine moved on, leaving the chauffeur behind.

The limousine pulled up beside us on the left. I sank deeper into the seat, fearful that Karp might look over and see me. But he kept his eyes straight ahead. Sitting behind the wheel of the Rolls-Royce, he looked like any handsome, distinguished bureaucrat, lost in distinguished bureaucrat's thoughts.

The light changed. Karp turned left and started cross-town. We followed.

Once again, I was musing upon the possible contents of Karp's dispatch case. "What if there's five pounds of heroin in that dispatch case?" I asked. "What would be its street value?"

"Pure stuff? About two million."

"Jesus," I murmured, "we're in the wrong business."

"Times like this, I know I am."

Chico was griping simply from force of habit. In fact, his

whole attitude had changed. His expression was serious and intent. He knew, as well as I did, that we were onto something.

The limousine crossed Central Park and kept on going all the way to the river. It turned up the Henry Hudson Parkway. We stayed on its tail, maintaining a discreet distance of fifty yards.

We passed Morningside Heights, then Harlem. At Fort Tryon Park, the limousine turned off the parkway and went through an underpass. Chico, caught unprepared, almost missed it and had to turn quite sharply.

We found ourselves on an uphill road that passed between the stone walls of a ravine. "Where are we going?" Chico asked perplexedly.

"The Cloisters," I replied. "Haven't you ever been here before?"

"Ashamed to admit it. Never have."

"I thought all photographers were art lovers."

"Yeah. But the medieval stuff doesn't turn me on."

The road curved and we came to an open stretch. Up ahead, at the top of the hill, we saw The Cloisters, a pseudo monastery of a museum, perched high above the Hudson. Its campanile, a rectangular bell tower the color of light earth, was silhouetted against a pale-blue sky.

The limousine parked in front of the museum. We slowed down to about five miles an hour, waiting to see what would happen next. Karp got out of the limousine and, carrying the dispatch case, started down one of the paths that circled around the hill.

We parked a few yards away from the limousine. I quickly got out of the car. I was excited and my impulse was to chase after Karp at once. My hunch had worked out, and I didn't want to delay and risk losing the pay-off. But I had to wait while Chico got his equipment out of the car.

I glanced around. The hilltop seemed almost deserted.

Two young Japanese men, with cameras hanging from their necks, waited at the bus stop; a guard stood by the dogwood trees near the entrance of the museum; otherwise, there was no one in sight. Only one other car was parked in the parking area, a shiny new Buick.

After a few moments, Chico was ready; he had his equipment—a Nikon, with a telephoto lens, and a two-degree spot meter. "Let's go," he said.

We hurried down the same path that Karp had taken. The path was carved from the rock face of the hill and it was lined on either side with tall maple trees. Above us, at the top of the hill, we saw protruding sections of the balustraded terraces of The Cloisters. Below us on the right, through the overgrowth on the steep hillside, we caught glimpses of the drab, old apartment houses of upper Manhattan.

The path was practically deserted, except for a few fat, complacent squirrels that just barely moved out of the way as we approached. Farther on, we came upon two young lovers, sitting on a grassy mound, caught up in a nonstop kiss. They didn't stir as we passed by.

We walked almost halfway around the hill, but there was no sign of Karp. I was afraid that we had indeed lost him, that somehow, in some way I couldn't figure, he had gotten off the path.

Then, as we came out onto the west side of the hill, we saw him. He was sitting with another man on one of several benches near a kind of rudimentary observation point. There was an impressive view of the Hudson and, across the river, the verdant cliffs of the Jersey Palisades; but neither of the men was paying any attention to the vista. They were conversing quietly, intensely. The dispatch case rested on the bench between them.

We stopped and retreated. Chico peeked around the bend, studying the situation. He looked disturbed.

"How's the angle?" I asked.

"Not good." Chico gazed up at the hillside. "Maybe if I can get up there."

He started up the steep incline. I followed after him, more slowly, since I was less sure-footed than he and the hillside presented an obstacle course of bushes and small trees sprouting their first spring growth. He clambered up to a clump of bushes near the crest of the hill, looked down on the other side, then turned back to me and nodded. I joined him and knelt beside him on the damp earth.

We were looking down at the two men at about a forty-five-degree angle, well off to one side, so that we saw Karp in profile and the other man, who was turned around on the bench to talk to him, in full face. This second man was a bit older than Karp. He had tanned, vulpine features and thick, dark hair; his hairline swooped down at the center of his forehead in a pronounced widow's peak. He was expensively dressed, in a dark business suit.

Chico raised the spot meter to his eye and got his light reading. He made the adjustment on his camera, then peered through the viewfinder. "I don't like the composition," he said.

"Screw the esthetics!" I whispered impatiently. "Shoot the goddamned picture!"

I heard the whirring of the shutter. "No good," Chico muttered.

There was a gradually swelling buzz in the distance. A police helicopter was coming down the river, skimming along only a few feet above the water. Karp turned his head to look at it and, for a moment, both faces were frontal to us. "Good!" Chico whispered. The shutter whirred again and went on whirring as Karp and the other man rose and shook hands. The other man picked up the dispatch case and walked away down the path. All the while, Chico was snapping pictures.

Karp turned and started back the way he had come.

"Let's get out of here!" I whispered. "Before he sees us."

Sliding, just barely keeping our footing, we hurried down the hillside. We ran back along the path toward the car.

2 "Don't know him," Jerry said. "I've never seen him before."

He was studying the best blow-up, the one that showed both Karp and the other man in full face. The man with the widow's peak showed up very distinctly. "Nope, I can't place him." He put the blow-up back on my coffee table, alongside the others. "Of course, that doesn't mean anything," he went on. "The Gero family has maybe four or five hundred soldiers. And I only know what half a dozen of them look like."

"You're sure he has to be someone in the mob?" I asked.

"Seems likely. A heroin delivery worth one or two million? They'd only trust one of their own to receive it."

"So how do I find out who this guy is?"

"Well, you could always go to the police," he said, straight-faced.

"Got any other brilliant suggestions?"

"I have a friend at the *Times*. Dick Bauer. He's their Mafia specialist. He might be able to identify this character."

"That's right, Jerry. Good thinking. After all this work, I'm just going to give away this story to the *Times*. What about your own contacts?" I asked. "Don't you know someone who could pin down this guy for us?"

He thought for a moment. "There *is* one man I know—" He broke off, then glanced at the prints on the coffee table. "Could I have one of these for a day or so?"

"No. These blow-ups stay with me. All of them."

"I want to show one to this man."

"Why can't I see him with you?"

"This contact is precious. Supersecret." He eyed me uncertainly, rather unhappily, as if he regretted having even hinted at the existence of his hidden jewel. "No one knows I have him."

"I'd never tell anyone."

"Maybe not. But a good contact is like a woman you love. You just can't bear sharing it with anyone else."

"Suit yourself," I said casually. "I guess it's not important enough to you. And your friend, Congressman Lampell, can have his ass whipped by the Mayor in the primaries."

Jerry sighed. "All right. I'll give this man a call. Maybe we can meet with him this evening. After he gets off duty."

"A cop?"

"What else?"

As he was leaving, Jerry said, "If I were you, I'd put some of these blow-ups in a very safe place. Like a bank vault. And I'd leave instructions where they should be sent in the event of my demise. It could turn out to be very valuable health insurance."

It was good advice, I knew, but I didn't happen to have a bank vault. For the time being, I would have to improvise a hiding place in my apartment. After Jerry left, I gathered up the prints and went into the study. I took down an old Brooks Brothers shirt box from the top shelf of the closet. In it, I had deposited all of the scarves, neckties, and handkerchiefs I had been given over the years and had never used. I opened the box and slipped the prints under the pile of stiffening accessories. I replaced the top and put the box back up on the shelf.

Half an hour later, the phone rang. It was Jerry. "Okay, it's set," he said. "I've just talked with my contact. He can meet us at ten tonight. That all right with you?"

"Fine. Where are we meeing?"

"The Inca. You know where that is?"

"It's down by the river, isn't it?"

"Yes. A nice, quiet, private place."

"What's your friend's name, by the way?"

"You don't need to know that," Jerry said. "See you." He hung up.

That night, at the appointed time, I put one of the blow-ups into my briefcase and walked over to the Inca. It was at the very end of West Twelfth Street; a waterfront bar-restaurant that featured half a dozen vaguely South American dishes. It was definitely off the beaten track and it was, I supposed, as good a choice as any for a clandestine meeting.

The place was nearly empty. Several slack-shouldered habitués were sitting at the bar, staring stupefiedly at a baseball game on TV. This seemed to be the extent of the action that evening. I passed through the bar and went into the dining room.

Jerry and his friend were already there, at a table by the last window. The contact was a big, silvery haired man with Celtic features, a bright-striped tie, and a suit that was cut full in the chest to make room for a shoulder holster. He had an air of authority about him, and, at a glance, I could see why Jerry prized him. He was clearly a substantial catch, something more than a mere junior-grade detective who had decided to tattle to the press.

"Don," Jerry said, "this is Joe." The big man rose and regarded me benignly.

"Good to meet you, Joe," I said, shaking his hand. I went along with the first name, even though I noticed that the initials on his monogrammed tie clasp were "D. L." As we sat, I inquired, "Should I call you Lieutenant Joe or Captain Joe?"

"Just plain Joe," Jerry said, with a warning note in his voice.

Joe turned his attention to the meat-and-beans dish he was devouring. He had been on duty twelve hours, he told me, in between mouthfuls of the stuff, and all he'd had was sandwiches. He was an honest cop, he went on, and he loved his work. He hated crooks, he hated crooked policemen even more, he hated crooked politicians most of all. He had been fighting the good fight for years.

But nobody appreciated his kind of cop. Hardly anyone even knew his name. He had killed two men in the line of duty. He had broken some pretty big cases.

"They could make a movie about me," Joe said.

Jerry sucked on his pipe thoughtfully and nodded.

By now, I had my suspicions as to the kind of lure Jerry had used to hook this big, inflated fish. Talk of a book contract, perhaps; the heady prospect of a block-buster and a big movie deal. Virtue coupled with vanity could be a dynamite combination. Nothing short of a .45 slug could stop it.

"Maybe there *will* be a movie," I said pleasantly. "You know, you look a little like John Wayne?"

"That observation has been made," Joe said placidly.

"Let's get to business," Jerry said.

I took the blow-up out of my briefcase. "You know what this is all about?" I asked Joe.

"Just what Jerry told me. You want me to try to identify some people in a picture, right?"

"And that's all he told you?"

"That's all I know."

I placed the photograph on the table before him. Joe looked down at it. "Hey, isn't that the guy who works with the Mayor? What's his name? Karp?"

"We know who he is," I said. "But who's the other one?"

Joe focused on the man with the widow's peak and now his expression was puzzled. "Is he a politician, too?"

"Maybe. Or maybe he's a crook."

"Same thing." After a moment, he shrugged and looked up. "No, I don't know him."

Disappointed, I picked up the photograph and was about to put it away.

"Wait a minute," Joe said. "Let me see that again." I

handed the photograph back to him. He held it and stared at it intently. "I know that face," he murmured thoughtfully. "I've seen him around somewhere. An ugly mug like that, you wouldn't think I'd forget it." His face brightened with sudden recognition. "Yeah! It was a couple of weeks ago. I was checking out a lead and I went into the Walrus. You know that place? Where the gay boys hang out? *This* guy was standing at the bar. I remember wondering what he was doing there. He didn't look the type."

I looked at Jerry uncertainly. "Isn't the Walrus—?"

Jerry nodded. "It's owned by Gabe Podesta."

3 After we left the Inca, I walked with Jerry up to Fourteenth Street and waited while he caught a cab. Then I started back down West Street. I walked briskly, in a hurry to get home. It was past eleven, a time of night when no one who was heterosexual walked those particular streets.

Quick, light footsteps were coming up behind me. They broke into a near-trot. A smiling young man in a madras jacket drew abreast of me. He had kohl on his eyelashes and invitation in his eyes.

"Nice night," he said.

"Wrong number," I said. "Keep going."

The smile vanished from his face. He accelerated into a near-trot again, hurrying on toward the mammoth truck trailers that lined the street a couple of blocks ahead. In the distance, I could see shadowy figures gliding around the parked trailers. It was in these that the nightly gay saturnalia took place.

Suddenly I noticed that a white Chrysler on the other side of the street was moving very slowly in the same direction I was going and keeping level with me. I had an uncomfortable sense of being watched. I began to get annoyed. Jesus, I thought, these gay boys just don't leave you alone. If they don't cruise you on foot, they cruise you on wheels.

I abruptly turned into Little West Twelfth Street. This street ran through the heart of the wholesale-meat district. At night, it was quite deserted, although not particularly dark. Naked light bulbs were fixed in the slanted wooden roofs that sheltered the sidewalks, and they provided some illumination. It wasn't a very cheerful street, but at least I would be left alone.

I walked on and crossed Washington Street. On the next block, I noticed that a section of the sidewalk in front of several warehouses was almost totally dark. When I reached that stretch of warehouses, I felt a crunching under the soles of my shoes. I was walking on broken glass. Someone had smashed the light bulbs.

A figure appeared from nowhere, a husky youth in a checked woolen shirt. He stood in my path, holding an unlit cigarette to his lips. "Got a light?" he asked.

I peered through the darkness at his features. He was baby-faced, not much beyond his teens. He certainly seemed straight enough. Probably a neighborhood kid, I thought.

"Sure," I said. I reached into my pocket for my lighter.

An arm whipped around my throat. At first, I was simply startled, and a bit puzzled. Then, with a shock of realization, I knew what was happening and I opened my mouth to shout for help. The arm pressed against my windpipe, choking off my cry. My hands went numb and the briefcase slipped from my fingers. I heard the thud as it landed on the pavement.

The boy removed the unlit cigarette from his lips. Unhurriedly, he drew back his fist and considered my midsection. My heart was pounding, I was strangling, but still I tried to brace myself, tense my muscles. He drove his fist into my stomach. My reflex was to double over. But the arm was tight around my throat and I could only convulse helplessly, gagging, pinned in an upright position. The boy studied me for a moment, dispassionately choosing another spot. His next punch hit me in the mouth.

There was a bright, white flash inside my head, then a shooting pain in my face. The pain made me hyperalert; it focused me. The taste of blood was in my mouth, but I concentrated totally as I maneuvered my right foot, feeling for a foot behind me. I found it and drove my heel down onto it. I heard a wounded, outraged cry and the arm around my throat released its grip.

I dove at the woolen-shirted one, grabbed him around the middle, and swung him off balance. I straightened up to run. Already the other man was lunging at me. I caught a brief glimpse of him—a sadly handsome, gray-haired man, who seemed much too old and dignified for this roughneck kind of work. Then my fist landed on the tip of his chin and he flew backward into the shadows.

I saw the young one's leg coming up. I was fully aware of it, momentarily fascinated by it, but I couldn't react in time. The tip of his boot sank into my groin. The sickening, honey-smooth pain welled up through me and I crumpled to the pavement.

I rocked on my hands and knees, groaning. A few moments went by; nothing more happened and I thought maybe it was over. Then I was kicked in the side of the head. I blacked out.

I may have been unconscious for only a few seconds. It might have been as long as a minute. I came to with a vague awareness that I was being carried somewhere. One pair of hands had me under the armpits, the other pair had me under the knees. It was rather comforting, and I felt no urge to resist; I didn't even open my eyes. After a few moments, I was lowered gently and the hands released me. I was stretched out on some rough tar surface. In my dazed state, it took me a couple of seconds before I realized I was lying in the middle of the street.

I heard the swelling hiss of a car approaching. I turned my head and opened my eyes. A white Chrysler was bearing down on me. In a desperate contortion of my whole body I flopped to one side. The Chrysler rushed past me, so near that I felt the wind of its passage and smelled the stench of its engine. Its left wheels passed directly over the spot where my head had been.

There was a screeching of brakes. I struggled to my hands and knees. The Chrysler had stopped. Now it shifted into reverse and started back toward me. I willed myself to rise to my feet. But a sudden upsurge of nausea robbed me of all strength. Something inside wanted me just to curl up and let the machine have its way with me.

I heard a shrill whistle. The Chrysler halted, only a few yards from me. Then it lurched forward and sped away. I had a blurred impression of two men running off down the street.

A few seconds later, there was the whisper of tires. A car had come to a stop behind me. I was powerless to turn my head. But I could see the spectral red flash on the tar surface, the reflection of the whirling red light of a squad car.

I let go then. I lay face down on the street and passed out.

4   At St. Vincent's, a weary, mildly bored intern checked me over. He found no broken bones or internal injuries. I had a bruised groin, a cut lip, and a lump on my head. He told me I could go home. I dressed, picked up my briefcase, and left.

When I came out into the waiting area, I saw that the two policemen had already gone. I wasn't surprised; they hadn't seemed too deeply interested in the episode. As far as they were concerned, it was an ordinary mugging, and I had said nothing that would have given them any other impression.

I felt a sudden pang of anxiety and I opened my briefcase. The blow-up was still there. They'd had it under their noses, the bad guys and the cops, too, and they had missed it.

When I got home, I doubled-locked the door and went around to make sure the windows were locked. I poured myself a drink, downed two Tuinals, took off my clothes, and got into bed. I propped myself up with pillows—my head ached less when I was in a sitting position—drank the Scotch, and relived my night's experience. I heard the ice cubes rattling in the glass and I realized my hand was shaking. I hadn't been particularly afraid while I was being beaten up, or when I was almost run over, or immediately afterward. But now— I had to admit it—I was frightened, frightened as hell.

The next morning, I phoned the U.S. Attorney's office and asked for Zanelli. I knew he might be involved in the conspiracy, too. But I had only my suspicions, and I couldn't afford to be paranoid. If he happened to be an honest official, I needed his help, needed it desperately.

The operator rang through to him and a crisp voice promptly came on the line. "Zanelli here."

"Hello, Mr. Zanelli?" I began. "This is Don Skelton."

"Yes, Mr. Skelton. What is it?"

"Well, I had something very disturbing happen to me last night. I was almost murdered."

"Oh?" There was no surprise in his voice. "How?"

"Some hoods in a car tried to run me over."

There was a brief silence. "I warned you, Mr. Skelton. I warned you you might get hurt."

"That's true, Mr. Zanelli. But I didn't call you just to hear you say 'I told you so.' "

"What do you want? Sympathy?"

"Look, Mr. Zanelli, give me some protection. Please. Give me a bodyguard or something."

"Why should I do that?"

"So I can finish this job. Then, when I'm ready, I'll turn over all my information to you."

"We don't need your information or want it."

"For Christ's sake, I'm a citizen of this country and I have a right to stay alive!"

"It is not in the taxpayers' interest to go to the expense of keeping you alive," he said coldly. "I've already told you what you should do—don't write that story. And now I'll give you another piece of advice. Get out of town and stay out. Because, if you don't, I can't guarantee *anything* for you. Those people may miss once. But they never miss twice." He hung up.

If I had had any question about Zanelli, it seemed to be answered. That last statement sounded more like a threat, one that could have been voiced by Aladino Gero himself. I wasn't up against just a few crooks, I now realized. I was bucking an elaborate conspiracy.

I sat there by the phone, thinking it over. Then I reached for the phone book and started to look up a name. If nothing else, I had come to one conclusion. I had no business tangling with the Mafia. I wasn't even *interested* in the Mafia.

Gangsters, for me, were like cockroaches. If I put two or three of them out of circulation, there would be three thousand ready to take their places. Organized crime would endure as long as society craved drugs, whores, and dice games. The battle against it was hopeless, and it wasn't my battle, anyway.

But Elliot Karp was something else. He was my assignment. I could forgo the Mafia, but I wasn't about to lose him.

One was as ordinary and diffuse as vice; the other was particular and meaningful, like something in a fairy tale come true. There was a princess and her mad father who were bewitched and held captive. I was the only one who knew how to save them. If I didn't break the enchanter's spell, no one would. That was personal. That was a moral imperative. I just couldn't walk away from it.

I found the name I was looking for. I dialed the listed number. There were two rings, then a secretarial voice answered.

"Hello, this is Don Skelton," I said. "Is Gabe Podesta there? I'd like to speak with him."

eight

1   Sally had changed her hair style. It was the first thing I noticed about her—that, and the fact that she was very nervous.

"What happened to you?" she asked, staring at my swollen upper lip.

"Oh, this?" I touched it lightly, since it was still sore. "I was doing some heavy interviewing in the West Village. Does it ruin my beauty?"

"You've looked better," she said.

"Well, I've never seen *you* looking so pretty. I like your hair that way."

"Do you?" Sally patted her hair self-consciously. She was letting it grow longer; parting it in the middle, combing it back on the sides, the classic look. "I thought I should try something —different."

"Why not?"

After a moment, she asked, "Would you like some coffee?"

"Not if it's any trouble."

"I just made it. It's French coffee. From Schapira's." This was my favorite coffee bean from my favorite coffee merchant. "I still go down to the Village to get it. Let me heat it for a moment." She disappeared into the kitchen.

I looked around the apartment. It was a tiny walk-up—just one room, basically, that fused into a sleeping alcove—and you could take in the whole of it with a glance. I saw none of the usual clutter. Sally had tidied up for me.

She returned. She stopped in the center of the room and looked at me questioningly. "Where is it?" she asked. "Whatever it is you want me to keep for you."

"Here." I took the large envelope that I had been holding under my arm and offered it to her.

"Is this it?" She sounded a bit disappointed. "You were so dramatic on the phone—I thought you were going to give me the Maltese falcon or something." She pinched the envelope. "Pictures?"

I nodded. "And a letter. Three copies."

"What do you want me to do with this?"

"Just keep it, for the time being. But, if anything happens to me, open it. Then send a set of prints and a copy of the letter to each of these three addresses." I gave her a file card. On it, I had written the addresses of the New York office of the FBI, the District Attorney's office, and the U.S. Attorney's office.

Sally's expression was serious now, rather troubled. "Does this have something to do with Elliot Karp?"

"Maybe," I said vaguely. "And maybe it's some other story."

She gazed at me uncertainly. "Why me?" she asked.

"You're the only one I can really trust."

She looked at the envelope again, then shrugged. "Well, I hope this all turns out to be unnecessary."

"You and me both."

We were silent for a moment. "The coffee!" she said, suddenly remembering. She put down the envelope and the card and hurried into the kitchen.

I glanced around the apartment, searching for signs of change, for any small giveaway that something new had come into Sally's life, but everything looked pretty much the same; even the three ashtrays were still in their same places. They were empty and dully clean, and looked as if they hadn't been used since I had last flicked ashes into them.

I peeked into the sleeping alcove to see if the framed snapshot of the two of us was still on the dresser. It was a snapshot that Sally loved and I hated; she looked great in it, I looked like a foolishly smiling boob. But, against all logic, I hoped to see it now. It was gone. Well, what had I expected?

Sally returned, carrying two cups of coffee on saucers. I sat on the couch and she placed my cup beside me.

I sipped the coffee. She had sweetened it exactly to my taste, a level teaspoon and a half. "Umm, good," I said.

Sally smiled absently. I watched her as she drank her coffee. She had a special grace in the way she performed the small, ordinary actions. Her fingers nestled delicately around a cup, or any other object, caressing it rather than gripping it. I realized how much I had missed seeing her do the simple, daily things—setting a table, arranging flowers in a vase.

Casually, I asked, "What have you been doing?"

"Catching up on my reading," she answered. "Watching television." A bit wryly, she added, "The usual things that people do when they're unemployed."

"Been going out?"

"I have been tremendously in demand," she said. "There's been a different man every night."

"Well, that's terrific," I muttered grimly.

"Relax," she said, smiling slightly. "I haven't seen any-one in two weeks. When a guy calls, I beg off sick."

"That's not right, either. You shouldn't cut yourself off."

"You sound like my girl friends." She took another sip of her coffee and looked away.

After a moment, I asked, "Have you been looking for a job?"

"No, not really. There wouldn't be much point to it. I'm thinking of going away."

I tensed up inside. "Where to?"

"Oh, I thought maybe California."

"What's in California?" I asked.

"What's here?" she responded, with a wan smile.

I felt a sudden sense of helplessness. I hadn't allowed for this. I had assumed that Sally would always be there, some-where near at hand, to be reclaimed when the time came.

But it wasn't to be that convenient, after all. Sally had ideas of her own.

"If you do go away," I said, "stay in touch, won't you? Send me a number where I can reach you."

"Why would you want to reach me?"

"I just can't accept it," I said. "That we're finished."

She looked at me calmly and said nothing.

"Or is there no chance?" I asked.

"Not as long as you're part of this scene," she said. "Not as long as you are what you are."

"You want me to give up my work?"

"Oh, it's not the work as such." There was a touch of weariness to her tone, as if she had already thought too much on the subject and was reluctant to think about it now. "It's not a matter of being a journalist or anything else." She shrugged. "It's a matter of honesty, I guess."

"I'm under the impression that, whatever else is wrong with me, that's one thing I am. Honest."

"Not with yourself, you aren't. You're the most self-deluded man I know," she said quietly. "Take this thing you're doing with Elliot Karp." She glanced at the sealed envelope on the side table. "It *is* Karp, isn't it?" I didn't answer. "What have you found out about him?" she asked. "That he's a crook?"

"Among other things, yes."

"With all due respect, Don," she said, "the fact that a New York City politician is a crook is no great revelation."

"Maybe not. But graft is like cancer, you know? It's commonplace—but you just don't ignore it."

Sally shook her head. "If it were simply a matter of larceny, you wouldn't bother. It wouldn't interest you; you don't relate to it. When it comes to money—you're right—you're painfully honest. So why should you care if someone else steals? No, that's not it," she said. "That's not why you're risking your life to destroy this man. It's not because of the things in which you're different from Karp. It's all the things in which you're *alike*. It's what you see of yourself in him you want to destroy."

I kept my voice light. I even managed a smile. "Would you care to explain?"

"I shouldn't have to, Don." The weariness had come back into her voice. "You're one of the bright ones. You're one of the hip New Journalists who know all about human nature. You see your own ambition—your own ruthlessness, your own vanity, your own deceitfulness, your own hunger for making it at any cost—you see all this in a man and it sickens you, right? So you want to obliterate him, smash him—the way you would smash a mirror."

I sat quite still for perhaps thirty seconds. I felt resentful, at a disadvantage, because I could tell her nothing of what I knew, could give her no idea of what was at stake, not for myself, but for Senator Wren and Penelope.

But, at the same time, I was confused. Something in me recognized that what she had said was—in part, at least—

true. And, no matter how urgent my task, how noble my motive, this truth cast a shadow on all that I did.

I set down the cup and saucer and rose. "Don't lose that envelope," I said.

I went to the door and opened it. When I turned back, I saw that Sally had not moved. She was sitting in exactly the same position, with the same serious, self-contained expression.

"What if I woke up one morning," I said, "and I was a totally different person? What then, Sally?"

"Are we talking about miracles?" she asked.

"Not a miracle. Just getting together with myself."

She was silent for a moment. "Wherever I go, you'll know where I am. I'll make sure of that."

"That's all I wanted to know," I said. I went out.

2 From the outside, the Walrus looked more like an abandoned French restaurant—which, in fact, it was. It was still early in the evening, but the place was already packed. I made my way through the rough trade types by the door, muscular hustlers in tight blue jeans, and went to the one open place at the bar.

"Where can I find Mr. Podesta?" I asked the bartender.

He pointed to a closed door at the rear. "Just knock on that door."

I went to the indicated door and knocked. A high-pitched voice called out, "Come in." I opened the door and entered the office.

Gabe Podesta was sitting behind a desk. He was in shirt sleeves, but his conservative necktie was neatly knotted, and he looked businesslike and rather out of place in his own establishment.

"Mr. Podesta? I'm Don Skelton," I said.

"Yeah, I know who you are," he said impatiently. "Sit down." Gwen Cooper had been accurate enough when she described him as talking like an "angry old woman." Even this ordinary conversational opening was spat out in a shrill, peeved tone of voice.

I sat in the chair in front of his desk and placed my briefcase on my lap. Podesta regarded me warily. His face was toadlike, his neck was chubby; the flesh of it overlapped his snug collar. Like many short men, he sat very straight, with his head tilted slightly upward. The posture enhanced his natural air of belligerence.

"So what can I do for you, Mr. Skelton?" he asked. "You say you got something to talk to me about. Something that concerns—how did you put it on the phone?"

"Our mutual security."

"Our mutual security. Now, this is a big mystery to me, Mr. Skelton. We got no business interests in common that I know of."

"We're both interested in Elliot Karp," I said.

"We are?"

"You know Elliot Karp, don't you?"

"Sure I know him. I know all the politicians. I got clients who do business with the city, and it's my job to know them. But Karp—" He shrugged. "I've seen him a few times, but he's no big deal to me, you know?"

"If he's no big deal to you, then why couldn't I have just dropped by your law office? I got the impression that Karp was *so* special to you that you wanted us to talk someplace very private. Like here."

For the first time, he smiled; it was a small, game-player's smile. "What's the matter, Mr. Skelton? You feel uncomfortable here?"

"Not particularly."

"Straight people sometimes do. Makes them feel insecure about themselves, I guess."

"*You* own this place, Mr. Podesta. And if you don't feel insecure, why should I?"

His smile froze. It occurred to me that, considering the place and circumstances, questioning a mafioso's masculinity was not the wisest thing I could have done. His hand slipped into his pants pocket. I tensed as I waited to see what he would draw out.

It was his wallet. He leaned forward over the desk and unfolded it, displaying a photograph of a stout woman and three children, two teen-age boys and a pubescent girl. "My whole reason for existence," he said solemnly. He folded the wallet and put it away. "But I'm a tolerant man, Mr. Skelton. I want everyone to be happy. And if it makes gay boys happy to be with other gay boys, then, what the hell, I'll give them a place where they can meet. I get along with them and they get along with me. They know I don't water the booze and I don't let anyone bother them. And let me tell you this—" he pointed at the door and his voice grew husky with intensity— "some of the finest people I've ever known are standing out there right this moment."

"That may be so, Mr. Podesta," I said. "But I really didn't come here to discuss Gay Lib."

"No, that's right, you didn't. You came here to tell me that I'm interested in this man I hardly know. What other big news have you got to tell me?"

He was playing it cute with me, which was making it more difficult than I had anticipated. I realized that I'd have to go back to basics, establish the obvious before I went into specifics. "Mr. Podesta," I began, "I'm sure you're aware that certain allegations are made about you in the newspapers?"

His eyes narrowed shrewdly. "You believe everything you read in the papers?"

"Well, I write for newspapers sometimes, myself."

"Then you should know better than most. A writer's got

nothing to write about. So he makes up a few things," he said, waving his hand to emphasize the trivialness of it. "The kinds of things people like to read."

Delicacy was getting me nowhere. I decided I might as well be bold. "You mean, the Mafia is just an invention of the media?"

"The Mafia!" Podesta stared at me in astonishment. Then he laughed. "The Mafia is something my grandfather talked about."

"It's no longer around?"

"I don't know. In the old country, maybe."

"You don't know anything about the Mafia here?"

"Only what I see in the movies." After a moment, he said, "I think maybe *you* seen too many movies, Mr. Skelton."

"And someone like—Aladino Gero, let's say—doesn't know anything about the Mafia?"

"Aladino Gero is a fine American," he said, indignantly. "Take it from me, I know the man. He's a very successful importer of olive oil. Is importing olive oil a crime?"

"No, it's no crime," I murmured.

He pointed his finger at me accusingly. "Trouble with you, Mr. Skelton, is you're a bigot. You think everyone who's of Italian descent has got to be a gangster. You don't know anything, Mr. Skelton!" he said angrily. "All you know is what you see in the movies!"

Rather desperately, I tried another tack. "All right," I said, "then let's say this is a movie. Let's say this is a movie and you're playing the part of a—well, a lawyer involved in the rackets." I paused, half expecting another flare-up. "All right? Can I go on?"

"You're doing the talking," he said. "I'm not saying anything."

"Then if I were a character in this movie," I continued, "this is what I would say to you. I have evidence that you and your colleagues are smuggling heroin into this country. And I have evidence that Elliot Karp is a key figure in this operation."

If, in fact, it had been a movie, there would have been an interesting close-up at this point. Podesta's face, which had been animated enough before, turned absolutely stony. It was as if he had been transformed into one of those grumpy frog statues you sometimes see in gardens. After a long moment of silence, he said, "Even in a movie, you got to have proof."

I unlocked my briefcase. I took out the single blow-up I had brought with me and handed it to Podesta. He looked at it.

"A photographer and I tailed Karp when he got off the plane from Rio," I said. "We followed him up to The Cloisters. We were watching when he met your man and delivered the stuff to him. And we took pictures. In this blow-up, as you can see, both of them are easily recognizable. The authorities should have no trouble identifying your man."

Podesta glanced up at me. "You shown this to them?"

"No. No one has seen these pictures," I said. "But, if anything happens to me, a full set of them, with an explanatory letter, will go to the FBI, the District Attorney, and the U.S. Attorney."

Podesta nodded and said nothing. He studied the blow-up again. He seemed intensely thoughtful, but his expression remained impassive.

At length, he asked, "What do you want? Money?"

"I just want to be left alone," I replied. "I want to feel free to go ahead and write my story."

"And use this picture?" His tone was faintly incredulous.

"Not necessarily. If you guarantee my safety, I won't use the pictures. I won't make any reference at all to your—international activities. I'll try to keep you out of it entirely."

"Then where's your story?"

"I have another story," I said, "one that you yourself

may not know. You see," I went on, "Karp happens to be a
fraud. He's faked his employment background, his service
record, and his educational background." There was a quick,
surprised lift of Podesta's eyebrows. This was, in fact, news to
him. "That's the story I'll break," I said. "It should lose him
his job, and I'm afraid he won't be much use to you after that.
But your over-all operation will remain untouched. I can do
an entire exposé on Karp without even hinting at this other
thing." I paused. I had met with no resistance so far. So I
decided I might as well go for as much as I could get. "Oh,
there's something else I may go into. I may bring up the
matter of that variance on the Broadway property. I suppose
I *will* have to mention your name in that connection. And Mr.
Gero's, too. But I can't prove anything. It would only be an
innuendo." I smiled. "And, by now, Mr. Podesta, you must
have gotten used to innuendoes."

I waited. But Podesta simply went on staring at me. His
eyes were hard and unfriendly, and I began to feel appre-
hensive. I had taken a calculated risk, one based on a logical
consideration of all the factors. But now I was far from certain
that Gabe Podesta saw the matter as logically as I did.

"If you think it over, Mr. Podesta," I said, "I'm sure
you'll agree that this is the most sensible compromise. We both
lose something and we both keep something." I paused. But
still there was no response. "Is it a deal?" I asked.

Podesta looked at the blow-up once more. Then he rose.
"Wait here," he said. "I got to make a phone call."

He crossed to the door that led to the adjoining room. As
he opened it, I caught a glimpse of another office, larger and
more luxuriously appointed than the one I was sitting in. He
went into it and closed the door after him.

I could hear nothing from the next office. But I imagined
Podesta dialing the number. And I imagined the phone ringing
in Aladino Gero's Long Island mansion. The minutes went by
and I grew increasingly nervous. It would have eased my ten-

sion somewhat if I could have gotten up and paced around the office. But, for all I knew, I was being observed through a peephole, and I didn't want to give the appearance of snooping. So I sat where I was.

Finally, Podesta returned. "It's a deal," he said.

"Then I can go ahead? And no harm will come to me?"

"If you stick to our agreement, nothing will happen to you."

"I have your word for that?"

"You got my word—and I got your word. That's all we need, right?"

"Right." And I laughed slightly, feeling a giddy sense of relief. The whole thing had turned out to be easier than I had imagined. "Then I guess that's it."

"That's it," he said.

I rose. "If we have nothing more to discuss, I might as well go."

Podesta picked up the blow-up from the desk. "Can I keep this?" he asked.

"Of course," I said.

3 The next morning, I started writing my piece. I worked through the morning and into the afternoon, without stopping to eat. The phone was blessedly silent. When, at a few minutes past two, it finally did ring, I was almost grateful for the interruption. I was punchy with fatigue and overdue for a break.

In my groggy state, the voice on the phone didn't register with me. "Is this Don?"

"Yeah. Speaking."

"It's Elliot Karp."

I was instantly alert. "Oh, hello, Elliot. How are you?"

"I'm fine, thanks." His tone, as always, was velvety and cordial. "Listen, Don, I think we should get together. It's time we had a talk."

"Well, I've already interviewed you. I've got all I need."

"There are a few other things we could go over."

"Thanks, Elliot. But I don't want to take up your time."

"Let's cut the crap, Don." His voice was suddenly hard and businesslike. "You know what I want to talk to you about."

"All right," I said, after a moment. "I guess I can get together with you a little later. Around six? Are you free then?"

"Six will be fine."

"May I ask one thing?"

"Go ahead."

"Will this be just between you and me? Or will Gabe Podesta know about it?"

I didn't know what to expect; pretended bewilderment, perhaps, or indignation. There was a brief silence. Then Karp said, "As a matter of fact, Gabe suggested it."

"And has this meeting been approved by Aladino Gero?"

There was another silence, a longer one; it stretched on for several seconds. At length, Karp said quietly, "So I understand."

"I see." Actually, I didn't. It made no sense to me at all. "Okay, where should we meet?"

"Do you know where Valjean's is?"

"I've never heard of it."

He gave me the address. It was on East Eighty-fourth Street. "See you there at six," he said. "I'll meet you at the bar." He hung up.

I did no more work that day. Instead, I spent the remainder of the afternoon clearing up odds and ends, all the time puzzling over this latest development. Why had Podesta suggested this meeting to Karp? What was the purpose? Did it mean that he had told Karp everything, including the details of our agreement? In which case, was the deal off? Or was this a subtle trick intended to deceive Karp, to give him the impression that Podesta was still looking after his best interests? If it *were* a trick, what would Karp be hoping to accomplish?

At twenty minutes to six, I caught a cab uptown. Valjean's turned out to be a hopeful little French restaurant, one of a hundred like it in Manhattan that start up with a promise of "authentic" cuisine and never quite catch on. A cocktail lounge was at the front. There was no one at the bar, except for a matronly blonde who I assumed was the hostess. A postadolescent couple sat at one table, two rather mannish-looking women sat at another, and, at a third table, a glum man in a striped sports jacket nursed a bottle of beer. He was wearing an obvious curly wig.

I sat at the bar and ordered a Scotch. At five minutes past six, Elliot Karp arrived. He was rather formally dressed, in a dark-blue suit, small-dotted tie, and shiny black shoes, as if he might have been at a tony luncheon earlier in the day. "Sorry I'm late," he said. "I got delayed. How are you, Don?" He thrust out his hand.

I rose and shook it. His grip was as firm and friendly as ever. I found myself exaggerating the warmth of my own handshake and, at the same time, not quite meeting his gaze. I felt uncomfortable, as if I were giving him a Judas kiss.

Karp ordered a vodka martini on the rocks. While waiting for his drink, he made small talk. Penelope and he had discovered Valjean's—they came there from time to time—the steak béarnaise was terrific, and so on. His martini was served to him. He took a large swallow of it, then turned to me. "Ready to talk?"

"Sure."

"As I said," he began, "I talked with Gabe Podesta."

"And with Aladino Gero?"

"No." His voice lowered. "I've never met Gero. I've never spoken with him. I don't even know what he looks like."

"But you said that Gero approved this meeting?"

"That's what Gabe said."

"Podesta told you that Gero thought you should talk with me?"

Karp nodded. "Yes."

"Talk about what?"

He smiled. It was an easy, disarming smile. "Well, it looks like you've got something on me."

"Maybe." Guardedly, I asked, "What in particular do you think I've got?"

He was still smiling, but his eyes were wary. "You checked up on my background?"

"Yes, I did."

"And Gabe said something about a—certain variance. Do you know what he was talking about?"

"Yes, I know exactly what he was talking about."

"Then I guess Gabe was right." He looked down into his glass.

As I waited for him to say something further, I kept my expression bland to mask my edginess. But he didn't go on. That seemed to be it. He hadn't said anything about drug smuggling, or anything that hinted he knew of the incriminating photographs. Nevertheless, I was still uncertain exactly how much Podesta had told him.

"What I don't understand," I said, "is how they can know what's in my head."

"Oh, those guys always know," he murmured. "It's spooky." He looked up at me dispiritedly. "Maybe you talked too much to the wrong people."

My question was answered. Karp didn't know about my meeting with Podesta. The mafiosi were playing some kind of game with him. And I had let myself be drawn into this pathetic exercise.

It was distasteful. But I was there. And I had to go through the motions. "Okay, Elliot," I said, "so now you know what I know. Now, just what is it we're supposed to be accomplishing?"

He didn't answer me directly. Instead, he gazed at me silently for a moment, with something like concern in his eyes. "You don't make much money at your work, do you?" he said gently. "I mean, a free-lance writer's life—it's pretty rough, huh?"

"Oh, I make do," I said. "It doesn't take much to keep me going. A crust of bread—a piece of cheese—"

Karp stared at his glass again. Barely moving his lips, he said, "I've been authorized to offer you fifty thousand dollars." He waited, but I didn't say anything. "You'll be given a plane ticket to Geneva. The money will be delivered to you in cash there. You can put it in a Swiss bank account. No one will ever know." He looked at me. "What do you think?"

I laughed. "I think you're out of your fucking mind."

His face was blank. I couldn't tell whether I had angered him, surprised him, or simply disturbed him so deeply he couldn't react at all. At length, very mildly, he said, "I knew you'd say that."

"If you knew, why did you bother? Is this offer real? Or were you just testing my integrity?"

"Oh, it's real, all right," he said. "I'm sorry, Don," he went on. "This wasn't my idea. Podesta and Gero—they don't understand people like you. They have a low opinion of human nature. They think all men can be bought. They just don't realize, the way you and I do, that writers are morally superior human beings."

I thought I detected a subtle dig in that last fine phrase. And I replied in kind. "Most men *can* be bought, I imagine."

He nodded gravely. "It certainly seems that way." He looked thoughtful for another moment. Then he laughed suddenly, as if the absurdity of the whole thing had just occurred to him. "Don," he said, leaning toward me and squeezing my forearm, "I like you. I really do. I think we could have been good friends. In more normal circumstances."

I found his hand on my arm quite unpleasant. At that point, his clownish bonhomie seemed grotesque, and the mere touch of him made me queasy. And yet I sensed something oddly genuine in this attempt to make contact. He seemed to be reaching out to me in some way that went deeper than his foolish, banal words.

I moved my arm away. "Well, Elliot, these aren't normal circumstances. And I'm not your friend. You're a crooked politician," I said evenly, "and I'm about to ruin you."

The geniality faded from his expression. His dark eyes regarded me somberly. "You wouldn't be doing this at all if I hadn't gotten hooked up with a neurotic woman. You realize that, don't you?"

"Yes, I know all about you and Margrit Hivnor," I said. "And I have no illusions about Blake's motives."

"And yet you still think it's worth passing up fifty thousand?"

"I've been given an assignment. I have to do it on principle."

"You should learn to rise above principle sometimes," he murmured. He turned back to his drink.

A minute before, I had been feeling a little sorry for him, the hollow golden boy reduced to offering me a crude bribe. But now his cynicism irritated me. "*This* principle is important," I said. "Not to go along with the lies, but to see men as they are —ugly as they can be."

"Do men always seem ugly to you?"

"Maybe it's the circles I travel in. Anyway," I said, "it's my job to understand what's going on with a guy like you. And to help the public understand."

"How can you make anyone understand?" His voice was suddenly weary. "You don't understand it, yourself."

"Oh, I understand, all right."

He looked at me. "You don't understand it. You don't understand at all."

The flat certainty in his voice was unsettling. "I've figured out your game pretty well, haven't I?"

"There are games within games," he said quietly. "All you see is the bare surface. You're only seeing what you want to see."

After a moment, I said, "All right, then, I can still revise my piece. Would you care to make a statement?"

Karp gazed at me as if he were about to speak, or, at least, *wanted* to speak, to tell me some particular and important thing. But his handsome face froze helplessly. It was as if the residue of a lifetime of evasions, subterfuges, and deceptions was still there, blocking him, damming up the impulse to express himself directly and spontaneously to me.

The seconds went by and he remained silent. At the periphery of my vision, I saw that the man in the curly wig had risen and was walking toward us. His hand was reaching under his jacket, as if he were fumbling for a pack of cigarettes in his shirt pocket. He came toward us so purposefully that I thought he was about to ask us for a light. Annoyed at his bad timing, wanting to discourage him, I swung around and faced the bar.

Karp, too, turned back and huddled over his drink. "Don, give me time." His voice was low and urgent. "Give me two months. Then I'll tell you the whole story. Please, Don. I need the time."

He looked up and saw, reflected in the mirror, the man in the wig, the extended arm, the revolver. There wasn't enough time for surprise or fear. There was only one final second of recognition.

Then the bullet tore into the back of his skull. The impact lifted him off the stool and threw him forward against the bar.

I was on the floor, my eyes half closed in terror, waiting for the second shot, the searing pain. I had a blurred impression of trousered legs walking quickly away. Then something struck my arm hard. I looked to see what had hit me.

Elliot Karp lay beside me, his eyes turned up toward the gaping red hole in his forehead. His limp hand rested heavily on my forearm.

I screamed and rolled free of him.

nine

1 I have only the vaguest memory of the next few hours. I was in a state of shock, and the impressions that have stayed with me are blurred and distorted. I remember sitting in a squad room at a police station while two courteous, soft-spoken men interrogated me, one of them a captain of detectives, the other an assistant DA. But I have no clear idea how long it took, whether I was kept there for one hour or three.

The captain did most of the questioning. "You didn't tell anyone you were meeting Mr. Karp there?" he asked, for the third or fifth time.

"No one," I said. "I didn't talk with anyone. I didn't leave my apartment all day."

"But the killer knew. He was at the restaurant, waiting for you."

"Yes, he was. I suppose Mr. Karp must have told someone. At his office, or somewhere else."

"We'll ask around," the captain said. "We'll find out if he did."

"Look, you don't think I set him up, do you?"

"We're not suggesting anything, Mr. Skelton," the Assistant DA interjected soothingly.

"I hope not," I muttered. "Jesus, I hope you don't think that!"

In the brief silence that followed, their eyes held on me.

"You were writing about who again?" the captain asked.

"Penelope Wren." I had the answer set by then, and I patiently repeated it, word for word. "I was interviewing Mr. Karp to get more background. Anecdotes. Human-interest touches."

"About Penelope Wren?"

"Yes. The man *is* her husband, after all." I stopped, then, dully, corrected myself. "Was."

Finally, it was over. "We'll be calling you, Mr. Skelton," the Assistant DA said. "In the next day or two, we'll want you to come down to headquarters and answer a few more questions."

A police escort led me out of the station. My colleagues of the press were standing on the sidewalk, waiting. In the few seconds they had to get at me, they barraged me with questions. I disregarded them, as I would have disregarded the yapping of small dogs.

As I was about to get into the squad car, I heard a familiar voice yelling, "Hey, Don! It's me! Jerry!"

I turned. Jerry Gutman was at the back of the pack, standing on tiptoe to make himself seen by me. "Was it those people we know?" he shouted.

I stared at him. I realized that, in that moment, Jerry wasn't my friend, my fellow worker, or even my fellow human being. He was a pure reporter, without friends, without feelings, a piece of equipment programmed to collect information. And, now that I found myself at the other end, I felt the same mingled disbelief and distaste I had so often seen in the expressions of my subjects.

I turned back and got into the squad car. "Don! Don!" Jerry was yelling. "I'll call you!"

When I got home, the phone was ringing. I let it ring until the answering service picked up. In a few minutes, it started ringing again.

By then, I had made my decision. When the phone was silent again, I went to it and dialed the number of a car-rental place. I reserved a car for immediate use. Then I phoned Gurney's Inn in Montauk and booked a room. That done, I sat at my typewriter and quickly typed a note, explaining that I was leaving town on urgent business, but would return in three days and would then be available for all questioning. I put the note in an envelope, typed out the address of Homicide Squad, Manhattan North, and attached a special-delivery stamp.

I knew it wasn't the smartest thing I could do. If the police had any suspicions about me, this would only serve to increase them. But I had an article to write. I needed privacy and uninterrupted quiet.

Anyway, what did I have to worry about? I was innocent. I hadn't done anything wrong. Still, there was a knot of anxiety in my stomach, and I felt all the sickening uneasiness of a guilty man.

As I sped through the night on the highway, following the white line toward the far tip of Long Island, my head began to clear. My thoughts at last were able to focus on what had happened. I went back over it, trying to understand it.

Aladino Gero had ordered the murder, of course, wanting to rid himself of the weak link that Karp had become. But there were a dozen other possible times and places for the murder; it didn't have to occur while I was sitting at Karp's elbow. Gero and Podesta, I decided, had deliberately staged the murder to have maximum impact on me, to terrorize me into silence.

If that were so, they had miscalculated. As Karp had said, Gero and Podesta didn't really understand journalists. They didn't understand the obsessive moth creatures that we were, fascinated by the flame, drawn ever closer to it. Karp's murder had made this one of the most sensational stories of the decade. Now, more than ever, I had to get it all down on paper. It was a matter of compulsion; I couldn't have kept myself from doing it.

My room at Gurney's Inn was an ideal writer's nook. From my window, I could look down a landscaped hillside at ocean breakers tumbling onto an immaculate beach. After a few hours' sleep, I woke to the cries of sea birds, a glorious dawn, and went immediately to my typewriter and started the article over again.

I set out to tell the whole story, excluding nothing. I understood the implications of it. Strictly speaking, Gero and Podesta had not violated our agreement. Podesta had promised me my life, but he had said nothing about sparing Karp. That was the fine point I had overlooked. So now, if I published the story, I would be the one who was reneging on the deal. And my life would be forfeit.

Yet I went ahead. The thing had gone beyond any sordid bargain I might have made with a Mafia boss. I felt responsible for Elliot Karp; I felt responsible for him in death as I never had when he was alive.

All right, he had allied himself with killers, had profited from a dangerous racket, and he might have come to a bloody end, sooner or later, anyway. But that didn't get me off the hook. Karp had been murdered at a particular time, at a particular place, and his hand had lain on me in the moment of his death. I had my share in it. I had participated. And now I couldn't let his death be reduced to something meaningless, nothing more than a clever, winning trick played by a foxy gangster. There had to be retribution. My article would be the instrument for that retribution.

For three days and nights, I worked almost nonstop, living on snacks, hardly ever leaving the room. My only contact with the world was the morning paper. It kept me informed of the progress of the Karp case. Or, rather, the lack of progress. The murder had all the earmarks of a professional job, the work of an expert hit man. But there was no known motive for a gangland execution of such a respected public official.

I read about the last honors paid to Elliot Karp. It had been Karp's desire that his funeral rites be in accordance with the customs of the Jewish faith. His widow, Penelope, obeyed his wish. At the funeral, the Mayor gave a long and eloquent eulogy.

The fourth morning, I typed the final words of the piece. I put down three asterisks, my usual coda, and stared numbly at the last page for a few moments. Then I glanced at the clock. It wasn't yet nine. I could get back to the city by noon, have time to deliver the article, and then report in to the police.

The traffic was light, there were no delays, and I returned to my apartment at a quarter to twelve. I took the manuscript out of my overnight bag and put it on the desk. Then I went to the phone and checked in with the answering service.

The operator recited a long list of callers. There was Jerry Gutman, of course; and, as I expected, Blake Hivnor had called every day.

When she finished her recitation, the operator said, "Someone else called a few times. A woman. She wouldn't leave her name."

"Did she sound young or old?"

"Young."

"What kind of accent?"

"Classy."

"Thank you." I hung up.

I remembered Penelope as I had last seen her, the toy panda clutched in her arms, her hostile stare, her dangerous smile, and once again I was suffused with a sense of uneasiness. *I don't want to see you again,* she had said. But the situation had been different then. Her husband was still alive.

The phone rang. I picked up the receiver.

"Don, where have you been?" Penelope's voice was tense, demanding.

"I've been out of town," I said. "Have you been trying to reach me?"

"Yes. Yes, I have."

There was a silence.

"Penelope, I—I'm sorry. You don't know how sorry I am."

"Yes, I know," she said quietly.

"I wanted to call you or write. But I didn't want to disturb you. And I—" I trailed off helplessly. The conventional phrases sounded inadequate and foolish now. Nevertheless, I felt compelled to say them. "Is there anything I can do?"

"I want to talk with you," she said. "As soon as possible."

"Of course, any time."

"Are you free this afternoon?"

"Yes. Where do you want me to meet you?"

"I'm not in the city," she said. "Ernest will come by for you. Two o'clock?"

"Two o'clock," I said.

She hung up.

2 The sanitarium had been somebody's country mansion once. From the outside, it looked like a Tudor manor house. Inside, it was a peculiar hybrid of oak-paneled elegance in the waiting room and institution-green everywhere else.

Ernest led me down the main hall toward the open French doors at the rear. Through the doorway, I could see a section of sunny, fairy-tale landscape, with dogwood trees in bloom and rosebushes.

Ernest stopped when we came to the doors. "Straight ahead down the path," he said. "She's waiting for you."

I went outside. It was a very large garden, bounded on two sides by high, red brick walls and, at the far side, by a cliff edge. Beyond it and hundreds of feet below, lay the river. It was a clear day and, across the Hudson, I could just barely discern the buildings at West Point.

I started down the path rather apprehensively. I was still completely in the dark as to the reason Penelope wanted to see me. On the way up, I had tried to question Ernest, but the chauffeur had responded only in terse, unhelpful monosyllables.

I passed a very old lady who was dozing in a wheelchair. A white-coated orderly stood stolidly behind her. A few yards away, a gaunt young woman in a flowered dress moved trance-like among the trees. Up ahead, near the end of the path, a man in a bathrobe and a girl in a bright spring frock were sitting in garden chairs on a stretch of lawn by the cliff edge.

The girl turned her head, looked back at me, then rose. It was Penelope. She cut across the grass to the path. She walked swiftly toward me.

"Don, I'm so glad you came." She was unsmiling, but, graciously enough, she held out her hand. "I hope this hasn't inconvenienced you?"

"Not at all," I said. "It's a beautiful day. It's good to be out of the city."

It seemed a little weird to be standing in that idyllic country garden, making small talk with the widow of Elliot Karp. But already I felt more at ease. I had expected something worse than this cool courtesy.

"We have lots to talk about," Penelope said. "But, first, you must say hello to my father."

"Certainly." I took a step to continue on down the path.

"Wait a minute." She put her hand on my arm and stopped

me. "I'd like you to do me a favor." She lowered her voice slightly. "I want you to tell Daddy that you've just seen Elliot and he's fine."

"What?" I stared at her uncomprehendingly.

"He doesn't know what's happened. We didn't think it would be a good idea to tell him. He's not completely well yet." She glanced quickly over at the man in the bathrobe. He hadn't turned; he was still sitting with his back to us. "But, you know —he's a very sensitive man—I think he suspects something's wrong."

I nodded. "All right. If you want me to."

We walked to the end of the path and crossed the lawn to where James Wren was sitting at the cliff edge. He turned half-way around in the wrought-iron chair and looked at me with a kind of genial wariness. His expression was questioning and I was pretty sure he didn't recognize me.

"Daddy," Penelope said, "you remember Don Skelton, don't you?"

"Of course," he said instantly. He still had the reflexes of the practiced politician. "How are you, young man?" He reached up to shake my hand.

"I'm fine, Senator." I squeezed his hand lightly. It felt cold and frail. Wren had lost a great deal of weight and he seemed wispy within the folds of the plaid bathrobe. His hair had grown out to the length of a close crew cut. I could see, beneath the new growth of white hair, the pink scars on his scalp, still-visible reminders of his self-mutilation.

"Come up from the city to visit us, have you?" he said.

"Yes, I just dropped by." I paused. Penelope was gazing at me expectantly. "Oh, by the way, I saw Elliot this morning. He sends his best."

"Oh?" I sensed his uneasiness. He tilted his head to one side and regarded me shrewdly. "And how is he?"

"He's fine. Very busy."

"Yes, I assumed he was busy. He hasn't been up here to see me for a while."

"Well, you know how hard he's working."

Wren nodded. "He's a worker, that boy. And ambitious. He's going to have to watch it."

"Watch what, sir?"

"He's got to be careful he doesn't seem *too* ambitious. Once you've got the smell of ambition on you, all kinds of people start lying in wait to bushwhack you."

I glanced away uncomfortably. "I think Elliot can look out for himself."

"We all need help. No one can do it on his own." He pursed his lips thoughtfully. "I think it's time he got out of city politics. There's no future in it. They asked me to run for mayor once," he went on. "I told them no, thank you. If I'm going to fall into a cesspool, I'll pick one where I've got a fighting chance to crawl out again."

I laughed politely. I gathered this was one of his set jokes. "You think Elliot should run for national office?"

"Not yet. He needs more experience. A federal appointment." Wren considered it for a moment. "Yes," he said, finally, "when I get back to Washington, I'll talk to Jack about him."

"Jack?" I echoed.

"The President," he said.

"Will you excuse us, Daddy?" Penelope broke in quickly. "Don and I have to talk something over." She took me by the arm and drew me away.

We crossed the path and walked on toward a line of trees that extended almost to the cliff edge. A stone bench was near the trunk of the last tree. We sat on it.

We were silent for a minute. Penelope gazed down at the river. And I gazed at her. I couldn't help it—I had never seen her looking so extraordinarily beautiful. Perhaps it was the sunlight or the clear air or the reflected brilliance of the river; but there was an exquisite shading to her complexion, a translucence to her skin. City interiors didn't do her justice. Her loveliness, I realized, was a country loveliness.

At length, she murmured, "I wish you'd known him before."

"I wish I had, too."

"He was an exciting, wonderful man. Everyone looked up to him. He commanded any room he entered." She looked at me proudly. For a moment, she seemed almost childishly boastful, a little girl bragging about her magnificent father. "He wasn't just *any* politician. He did some great things."

"I know his record. Civil rights, fair housing—I've read all about it."

"Do you respect what he was?"

"I respect what he was," I said. "And I respect him now."

"Then I'll put his life in your hands," she said quietly. "You can kill him or save him. It will be up to you."

"I don't know what you mean."

Penelope folded her hands in her lap and looked down at the ground. She took a deep breath, as if she were trying to screw up her courage. But when she looked at me again, her expression was calm, her tone was matter-of-fact. "I'm about to tell you a story I've never told anyone before. And it won't be easy for me to tell it to you now."

"All right," I said. "I'm listening."

"My father is a gifted man," she began. "But there is one talent he lacks—a talent for business. And so when he had to take over Wren and Sons—well, nothing seemed to go right." She looked at me uncertainly. "I'm not sure if you know about all this—"

"Yes, I do. The company almost went under."

"It would have gone under—if Daddy hadn't done what he did. And thousands of people who had trusted in the firm would have been badly hurt. He was worried about *them*," she insisted. "He didn't care about himself."

"And what exactly did he do?"

"He needed to borrow a large sum of money. But, wherever he went, he was refused. The firm's credit wasn't good any more. Finally, when he had nowhere else to turn, he went to a—" She broke off. "I don't know what to call him. In the old days, you'd say 'usurer.' "

"A loan shark?"

"Yes. A loan shark," she repeated distastefully.

"How much did your father borrow?"

"Quite a lot. I really don't know how much." She gestured vaguely. "One million—two million—"

"Must have been a pretty big loan shark if he dealt in that kind of money."

"Yes. I believe he was rather prominent, in his own way," she said dryly.

"And so Wren and Sons was saved?"

"Not in the long run. But it made it possible for my father to pay the firm's debts and dissolve it honorably. And all those little investors were saved. As for Daddy himself—he was ruined. And he still had to pay off that loan—which, of course, he couldn't do. He could hardly pay the interest, much less pay back the principal."

"And so what happened?"

"This man—this loan shark—kept threatening my father. Until finally—" She paused uncertainly. "Well, I can only guess at what was said—how it was done. But it seems that it wasn't this man's money. The capital had been advanced by certain other individuals. And now this man told my father that something could be arranged. But Daddy would have to go and speak with the man in charge. And he did," she concluded.

"Who was the man in charge?"

Penelope lowered her eyes and was silent for a moment.

Then, very softly, she replied, "His name was Aladino Gero."

She looked up quickly to take in my reaction. She smiled faintly, bitterly, as if she were grimly satisfied by the surprise in my expression.

After a moment, I asked, "And an arrangement was made?"

She nodded. "Gero told Daddy that he could forget about the money. All he asked in return was a few small favors when he needed them. And, for a long time," she went on, "the favors were very small. Advice that any good lawyer could have given—some inside information on government matters—" She paused. Then, in a more subdued tone, she admitted, "And, yes, once or twice he did intervene for Gero's friends. But, all in all, it wasn't very much." Her smile was fleeting, as swift as a twinge of pain. "Just enough to put my father in Gero's power forever. Because now, you see, Gero had something on him. He could always let it be known that Senator James Wren was an accomplice of gangsters."

"How do you know about this?" I asked. "Did your father confide in you?"

"Not at the time. Nobody knew. It was later—when he started to break down. One night, he told me the whole story. He couldn't keep it to himself any more, he had to tell someone."

I felt confused. I had spent weeks clarifying a picture. And now the picture had gone suddenly out of focus. "Then I don't understand," I said. "How did Elliot get into this?"

"Don't you see?" The lines of anguish deepened in her face. "It was Daddy! It was Daddy who corrupted Elliot!"

She turned away and closed her eyes. She sat there quietly, head bent, hands folded in her lap, in a posture that suggested thoughtful repose, except that her hands were gripping each other so tightly the knuckles had turned white.

After a while, she opened her eyes and gazed blankly at

the river below. "Eliott was so naive!" she murmured. "He was a true innocent. He believed in magic. Magical secrets. Magical answers. And he revered my father. Not simply because he was a good man. But because he thought of him as some great magician who knew all the secrets. If Daddy said something should be done in such a way, Elliot accepted it. It was the way the great and powerful had always done it. And *he* would do it that way." She was silent for a moment. Then she looked at me again and, in a more casual tone, continued her story. "As I said, for a long time Gero didn't make any extreme demands on my father. Not until Elliot got the Urban Development appointment. Then he told Daddy that he wanted to do business with Elliot. My father was already in too deep. He had to agree to it. And so a meeting was arranged between Elliot and one of Gero's people, a man named Podesta. From then on, Elliot was trapped along with my father." She paused. Then, very softly, she said, "I think that that, more than anything, was what haunted my father—and what finally made his mind go. The thought of what he had done to Elliot."

"But what about you?" I asked. "Didn't you ever talk to Elliot? Warn him about what he was doing?"

"I didn't know until later. And, by the time I found out—" she shrugged—"I no longer cared about him."

"You had stopped loving him?"

"More than that. I had already begun to despise him. I saw him as the pathetic opportunist he was." After a moment, she went on. "To be honest, I don't think I ever loved Elliot. Oh, I thought I did for a while. But not really. I married him on impulse—against my father's wishes. And I never forgave myself for it."

"Then why didn't you divorce him?"

"I was considering it. But then Daddy and he became hopelessly tied together in this thing, and I was trapped, too. You see, I had to keep up a beautiful appearance—the perfect marriage, all the rest of it—so no one would guess that things had gone so terribly wrong. I had no choice. I had to protect my father."

Once again, it had come back to her father. *I had to protect my father.* It seemed to be her ultimate rationale, something that went beyond all other human needs. And a sudden suspicion sprang up in my mind.

"I'm curious about something," I said. "About something that happened to me." She looked at me, politely attentive. "Some of Gero's men tried to kill me. Was Elliot responsible for that?"

"No," she replied. "Elliot had nothing to do with it."

"Was it you?"

She barely paused. "Yes. After we saw each other that last time, I phoned Mr. Podesta and told him exactly what you had said to me."

"Didn't you realize that he and Gero might do something about it?"

"I assumed they would. Those people usually take action on such matters."

"Did it occur to you they might kill me?"

"Yes," she said. "I thought they might."

The calm in her voice chilled me. And I believed her, believed that she had wished me dead. And that, if I really had been killed, she would have felt no remorse. She would have appreciated my extinction as a necessity, nothing more.

Penelope seemed to read my thoughts and she smiled slightly. "I'm not a nice person, Don. If you've romanticized me, I'm sorry. The truth is I have very little feeling for people. I try to be a good mother to my child. I love my father. And that's all there is to me." Her gaze was open and candid and her blue eyes were, as ever, beautiful and mesmeric. But now I saw in them, not a mystery, but the cold desolation of her all but empty universe. "If I'm asking anything of you now, I'm not asking it for myself. I wouldn't. I know I'm not worth it."

"What are you asking of me?"

"Elliot is dead," she said. "Nothing you write can affect him now. But if you expose Elliot, expose what he did, my father will be exposed, too. Exposed to humiliation. Exposed to disgrace. All the great things he has done will be forgotten. And why, Don?" she asked, with quiet intensity. "What good would it do?" She looked past me. "He's no danger to anyone. Can't you see?"

I looked back at the shrunken man in the bathrobe, sitting at the cliff edge. Wren was hunched forward, staring down at the river, seeming to follow the course of some small boat.

I turned back to Penelope. Her expression, as she gazed at her father, was transformed with tenderness, the singular tenderness of her one particular love. "He's out of the conspiracy now," she said. "He's out of our world. He's found a home in the past. And I don't think he's ever coming back." Her voice dropped to a pleading whisper. "Please, Don. Let him end his life in peace."

3 Ernest dropped me off at the door. We parted wordlessly —we hadn't said more than three things to each other on the way back—and I went up the steps and entered the brownstone.

I climbed the inside stairway, still mulling over the story Penelope had told me. Preoccupied, I didn't notice anything out of the ordinary until I was actually standing before my apartment door. Then I became aware of the sound of footsteps within, of furniture being moved, and I saw that the door was slightly ajar.

My first thought was to race out of the house, go to the phone at the corner, and get the police there before the burglars could escape. Then it struck me that any criminals professional enough to pick my lock would be less noisy about their work. I realized what was really happening. Angrily, I threw open the door.

The first person I saw was Zanelli, sitting in the armchair, reading the manuscript of my article. The Brooks Brothers shirt box lay on the table beside him, the stack of blow-ups heaped on top of it. Two other men, in the shapeless suits of plainclothes detectives, were putting things back into place.

Zanelli barely glanced up at me. He seemed indifferent to my arrival.

"Do you have a search warrant?" I asked him.

Zanelli reached into his inside jacket pocket, took out a folded sheet of paper, and held it out.

"Never mind," I said.

He put the warrant back into his pocket and returned to his reading. He had just started my manuscript.

"Put that down," I said. "You have no right to read my private papers."

"Shut up," he said, without looking up.

"What are you supposed to be?" I asked furiously. "The goddamned Gestapo?"

Zanelli's head jerked up and he glared at me. "All right, Skelton," he said, putting aside the manuscript and rising, "suppose *you* tell me." He picked up the top blow-up and glanced at the pictured faces of Karp and the man with the widow's peak. "How did you get these?" he asked.

"With a camera. What else?"

He stiffened and his fist clenched. Instinctively, I stepped back a bit. I realized that Zanelli, for some reason, was possessed by rage; it was taking all his self-control to maintain even the semblance of the calm interrogator.

"Did you take these pictures yourself?" he asked.

"A friend of mine did. But I was there, too."

"Have you shown them to anyone?"

"No one."

"Are you sure?" His voice was quietly insistent. "No one else has seen any of these?"

Something about the intensity of his gaze was making me

very nervous. After a moment, I said casually, "As a matter of fact, I did show a print to someone."

"Who?"

"Gabe Podesta."

"Why?" It was a shocked whisper.

"To stay alive, that's why. It was the one thing I had on Podesta and his buddies."

Two men came out of the study. The one in front said to Zanelli, "We're through in there." He looked at me curiously.

I stared back at him, stunned. He was the man with the widow's peak.

Zanelli saw my reaction and smiled grimly. "Skelton, I'd like you to meet Mr. Robson of the Drug Enforcement Administration."

I felt suddenly nauseated. I sank onto the couch. "Oh, Christ," I whispered.

"They're his pictures, all right," Zanelli was telling Robson. "He and someone else took them. They must have tailed Karp from the airport."

He went on, filling in Robson, but I put my hand over my eyes and stopped listening. Why was he bothering to explain? I wondered dazedly. It was all so obvious—obvious even to me, now that it was too late.

When I looked up again, Zanelli and Robson were leaving. The other men were already out in the hall. Robson went out, with one last glance at me.

Zanelli paused in the doorway. "I'll be down in a minute," he said to the others. He turned back to me.

"He was working with you?" I asked.

"All the way," he said.

"From the beginning?"

"No. For the past year or so. We got on to Karp pretty early. We had enough to indict him. But he agreed to co-operate with us."

"And that dispatch case—?"

"It had tapes, photographs, documents. The latest evidence he had collected. He was giving it to Robson. But none of it is much good without *him*. Karp was our key witness. Without him, we don't have a case." He regarded me bitterly. "You've screwed things up beautifully, Skelton. Thanks to you, our man is dead, and a whole year of work has gone for nothing."

I looked away, avoiding his dark, accusing gaze. "Why did he do it? Was he that afraid of prison?"

"Elliot? He wasn't afraid of anything. He was the bravest man I've ever known."

"Not even of being exposed?"

"He would have been, anyway. Once we brought our case to court."

"Then why did he do it?" I asked. "Why was he so ready to risk his life?"

He thought for a moment. "Maybe he was a romantic," he said. "Or maybe he just wanted to do something useful for once."

Zanelli took a step to go. Then he turned back and pointed at my manuscript. "Put *that* in your story. Tell what that poor son of a bitch did. Someone should know."

4 The daylight was fading. It was past six, perhaps closer to seven. I had been sitting motionless at my desk for over an hour. I had been brought there originally by some vague impulse to revise. But the cover was still on the typewriter. The manuscript lay on the desk, untouched.

I looked at the manuscript more closely now. The margin of the first page was dented; Zanelli had gripped the paper too hard. I stroked the indentation with my fingertips, trying to smooth it. Then I smiled at the absurdity of it, that I should still be so protective of this useless, fatal piece.

But then, I had gone to unusual lengths to get this twenty-four pages of text. Among other things, I had killed a man. I had brought about his death as surely as if I had pulled the trigger myself. When you have spilled blood to obtain an artifact, it takes on a certain value, no matter what.

I heard someone coming up the stairs. It was a heavy step, unfamiliar, but I paid no real attention. I assumed it was someone who was visiting one of the upper apartments.

The footsteps stopped outside my door and there was a knock. I felt a chill of fear. Desperately, I tried to remember if I had locked the apartment door.

The knock wasn't repeated. I heard the door open slowly. Then the footsteps came across the living-room floor and approached the doorway of the study.

I bent my head and gripped the edge of the desk. Let it be fast, I prayed. Let it be fast as it was with Karp.

Someone was standing in the doorway. I turned quickly and looked.

It was Blake Hivnor. He was smiling. "Well, at least you're still alive," he said.

I let out my breath. Then I laughed with relief. "I wouldn't die without letting you know, Blake."

"I wonder. Writers! They never tell me anything." He came over to the desk and glanced down at the manuscript. "It's finished?"

"Almost."

Blake picked it up and looked at the first page. I was about to snatch it back from him. Then I thought, What the hell, let him read it. What difference does it make?

He went over to the studio bed and sat. He leaned forward, propping his elbows on his knees, and started to read my article. I lit a cigarette and watched him. He went through the pages swiftly, scanning the typescript with a trained editor's eye, his head moving back and forth as quickly and rhythmically as a metronome set at presto. Every so often, he murmured "good" or "beautiful," and even, once, "terrific."

In no time at all, he was at the two-thirds point. Looking at the pages upside down, I could see that he had reached my description of our adventure at The Cloisters. He looked up. "Where are those pictures?" he asked. He glanced over at my desk. They weren't there. I had put the blow-ups away in the storage cabinet.

"I'm not showing them to you," I said.

"Why not?"

"Because I don't want you to run them."

Blake squinted at me perplexedly. "Don, this is great copy. The best thing you've ever done." He smiled reasonably. "But we'll need those pictures."

"Yeah, it's great copy. The best thing I've ever done. And it also happens to be a crock of shit."

He studied me for a moment. Then he shook his head. "You didn't invent this. It all rings true. Elliot Karp was a fraud and a corrupt politician."

"Yeah, that's true. But I left out one important thing."

"What?"

"Karp was a hero."

"How so?"

"He was an undercover agent for the government. He worked with Gero and the others so he could learn about their heroin operation—crack it open. He risked his life to do it, and he almost carried it off—almost."

I caught the fleeting look of distress in Blake's eyes. I knew that this wasn't what he wanted to hear about the man he had hated so deeply. But, after a moment, the professional in him won out. "Interesting," he murmured. *"Very* interesting." He glanced through the last pages of my article. "Does that come near the end?"

"It's not there at all. I didn't write it."

He looked up at me questioningly and said nothing. He was waiting for an explanation.

But I had no intention of explaining. I knew it would be useless to tell him about James Wren, to try to re-create my afternoon at the sanitarium on the Hudson. Any appeal to Blake's sentiments would be a waste of time. Instead, I simply said, "I can't write the story. It would mean revealing my sources. And some of them are still undercover."

"There are ways of getting around that."

"There's *no* way of getting around it."

Blake pondered for a few moments. Then a peculiar half smile came onto his lips. He flipped through the first half of the manuscript. "Yes," he said softly. "Yes, that should work nicely."

"What should work?"

"We'll cut out all the stuff about the drug traffic. That's half your article. But it still leaves the faked background, the gangland connections, the graft." He shrugged humorously. "Half a loaf is better than none."

I stared at him. "Jesus, the man sacrificed his life!"

"There are no heroes," Blake said coldly. "Karp was a wheeler-dealer. And this was just one more deal."

I gazed at him puzzledly, not trying to fathom him, but trying to imagine what it felt like to be him, one of the most powerful men in media, maimed, oversimplified, a mere organism feeding on other organisms.

I picked up a fountain pen. "Let me have that back for a moment," I said, holding out my hand for the manuscript. "There are a couple of changes I want to make."

He hesitated for an instant. Then he returned the manuscript to me.

I put down the pen and picked up my lighter. The flame sprang up on the first try. I held the corner of the manuscript to the flame, held it there until the yellow fire started to crawl upward at a diagonal, leaving a trail of curling black paper.

I dropped the flaming manuscript into the wastebasket.

There were several crumpled sheets of paper at the bottom. They gave body to the blaze. Smoke billowed from the wastebasket and filled the study.

I looked at Blake. He hadn't moved, his expression hadn't changed. He regarded the blaze in the wastebasket as calmly as if it were a bonfire we were sharing on a cold night.

"I can see why Margrit loved Karp," I said. "He had an edge on you. A sense of honor."

He got up slowly, heavily. His eyes were blank, but the half smile remained on his lips. "You're finished, Don."

The words didn't apply. He was addressing a man who was, in fact, already dead. I looked into the blaze and watched the remains of that man dissolve in flame.

We were rendered into ashes, Elliot Karp and his killer. Now one of us could be reborn.